CRYPTID COLLECTOR

SAM M. PHILLIPS

CRYPTID COLLECTOR

WWW.SEVEREDPRESS.COM

This novel is a work of fiction. Names, characters, places and incidents are the product of the author's imagination, or are used fictitiously. Any resemblance to actual events, locales or persons, living or dead, is purely coincidental.

ISBN: 978-1-923165-46-5

1

HIMALAYAN FOOTHILLS, 1989

Tom stood on the edge of a precipice, a wide, barren valley stretching before him. The rocky ground looked like a torture device, points sharp and dirty. He quaked at the thought of crossing those fields, his feet already hurting in unconscious sympathy with his future self, unhappy as he slogged over them. But they were just the first in a series of trials to come, and hardly the most forbidding obstacle between him and his goal.

My father's goal, not mine, he thought, correcting himself.

Beyond that desolate field of sharp boulders were the jagged peaks of a distant mountain range. Snow covered them like a blanket, hiding their deadly secrets. The grey ridges of the highest mountain sliced down to the Earth like blades cutting into a continent.

That mountain was a killer, same as all its brethren, flanking it on either side like thralls around their liege lord, their swords as yet sheathed in snow, but soon to be drawn, ready to strike Tom and his father down for daring enter their lands. What those deadly mountains were protecting, he didn't know. At least, he pretended not to know, to not remember the word his father repeated like a prayer, over and over.

Yeti.

"Ten feet tall or more," his father would say expansively, his eyes flashing in the flames of the campfire each night like a man in the grip of gold fever. "Some say it has brown or red hair, even black. But don't you believe them. It's white like the snow for camouflage—that's what makes it so elusive to track down. It explains the lack of photos too, but that could be because it shuns civilisation so completely. Yes, the yeti is a cunning creature."

His father would get thoughtful for a moment, staring into the fire, and then rouse himself, as if the monster were there before him in all its terrifying glory. "It has eyes like the burning embers of this fire, and huge teeth like a lion's for eating flesh. You wouldn't want to meet it on a cold, dark night like this, mark my words, for the monster has the bestial bloodlust of a wild animal. Does it hunt with tools? Nonsense, it has no need for the weapons we use."

He'd pick up a rifle and shake it in the air, then toss it down in scorn before continuing, raising his meaty hands. "It uses these. With its mighty clawed fingers it can kill even a Himalayan cougar, easy as you please. I've seen the corpses, ripped apart in bloody hunks. But the yeti's hunger is its weakness. You'll see. We'll get the drop on it when it's busy munching on the bones of its prey."

These details changed in each retelling of the tall tales, and were often contradictory. Tom knew his father had never seen a yeti himself, only heard the stories the Sherpas told, which he repeated each night as if they were his own, changing and inventing details wherever it suited him.

Tom didn't know why he bothered. Perhaps they were like a mantra, a meditation to focus his father's will on his prize, or a spell which could conjure the beast out of the snowy mists. Whatever the case, Tom hoped they would deliver the yeti to his restless father soon. Then at least they could go home, away from this biting cold, chilling his bones—away from this anxious terror, lingering in his guts like a lump of ice.

An involuntary shiver ran down his spine, a ghostly finger of fear finding each vertebra in turn and sending phantom sensations through his nervous system. A boy of fourteen shouldn't have to know about such things, shouldn't have to face things as terrible as numbing cold and mortal terror. The thought of such a monster had provoked a round of bedwetting his father was trying to beat out of him, deathly embarrassed by the boy.

"He's just sick, you know how it is, with this dirty food and filthy water," his father would say to the Sherpas in explanation, somehow oblivious or uncaring that the food and water had been provided by these same men. Then, in seeming contradiction to his reasoning, his father would smack Tom around the back of the head, curse him out.

Then they would go through the humiliating ritual of hanging out the sleeping bag, drenched in stinking urine, hoping the cold sun or the freezing winds would somehow dry it before they had to head on to the next camp. Invariably, Tom would have no choice but to climb into the still wet sleeping bag of a night, the horrid stench of it reminding him of his shame. He'd grown to associate his fear of the yeti with this acrid urine smell.

In his dreams he always tried to remain downwind of the yeti's lair, always failed. Each night the monster would stalk him like a dread shadow across the bright white snow. The horrifying roar of the monster would loosen his bladder, and the bedwetting cycle would repeat. He'd wake up drenched, not all of it pee, the cold sweat on his brow transferring the fear he felt from the dream world into reality.

Breathing heavily, he'd lie there, soaking wet, in the dark. Knowing the yeti was coming for him, he'd wait for the cold, grey light of day to peek over the horizon. It happened last night. It happened every night. The day did not dispel the fear. It provoked it, the mountains doing little to comfort him. They stood like sentinels between him and a manhood which felt elusive, something his father would not bestow upon him, not until he helped bring in the yeti, mounted its head on the wall of the family home.

He watched those mountains now. They looked so huge, it seemed impossible they could even find the beast, let alone best it. Even if they found it, would they be equal to the task of bringing it down? The stories his father told did not engender confidence. Death was closer than any of them realised.

We're not the hunters. We're the prey, thought Tom, as he stood on that precipice, overlooking the valley. He felt the pull of gravity, tugging him forward to fall to his doom, dashed on the rocks below.

And we're too stupid to even run away.

2

"Careful with that rifle, boy. Do you know who it belonged to?" Tom's father shouted over his shoulder as he paced out the target across the rocky field. Tom fought down the urge to lower the weapon, pinch the bridge of his nose in frustration.

Of course I bloody do, you tell me every single time I hold the damn thing.

"It's Lord Kitchener's rifle," his father answered for him. "Cost me a pretty penny, but totally worth it. That's history, boy."

Tom very much doubted the rifle had ever belonged to Lord Kitchener. His father might be rich, easily able to buy such a historic artefact, but that didn't mean he wasn't also a born sucker, easily duped by a compelling tale of heritage. The weapon didn't even seem old enough— the wear on it could easily be faked with a rough cloth. But his father believed what he wanted to believe, a story worth more to him than anything of actual, tangible value—a common curse of the ultra-wealthy.

I wonder if that's why he chases after monsters which might not even be real. The world of human affairs already in hand, the game of capitalism conquered, all that's left to overcome is the unknown.

Tom was well aware that this was what brought most wealthy tourists to Mount Everest. They wanted a new challenge, to test their mettle against the mountain itself, an indomitable foe few had faced and lived to tell the tale.

So why can't my father be content with simply climbing the damn thing like those other bastards? Why does he have to hunt its most elusive resident instead?

Tom already knew the answer to this.

Because men have already conquered the summit, but no one has conquered the yeti.

He worked the well-oiled bolt of the Lee-Enfield .303. At least the weapon was looked after and served its purpose—he'd lost count of the prey his father had taken down with it, always gloating afterwards with his cry of victory like the catchphrase of a dated cartoon character.

"Hoo roo," his father shouted now to get Tom's attention, using that same annoying turn of phrase. A bottle was propped on a rock at one hundred yards.

He's feeling optimistic, thought Tom.

"Or at least keen on embarrassing me," he said to himself, hefting the weapon and planting the butt in tight against his shoulder. The Lee-Enfield wasn't a light rifle. The iron sights danced around the bottle as he squinted along the length of it, his scrawny arms unable to keep the rifle steady. The longer he held it up, the worse his aim got, and it wasn't improved by his father shouting at him.

"Come on, junior, today if you please," he said, his mildest taunt, which escalated into name calling and furious swearing as Tom failed to take the shot, his arms shaking now from the strain of holding the rifle up. Eventually he gave up, decided to pull the trigger as the sights floated vaguely past the bottle. There was an anticlimactic click, deafening loud in Tom's ear as his mind expected to hear a loud bang.

"It would help if you load the damn thing, you useless bugger," his father said, scrunching up his woollen beanie and tossing it down on the ground.

Tom quickly and mechanically lowered the rifle, pulled a clip from his pocket, clicked it into the magazine catch. The bolt stuck a bit this time as he worked it, as if reluctant to let him use an actual bullet, aware somehow that his heart wasn't in it, or perhaps of the deadly consequences of the Rubicon he was crossing. He cursed himself out for a weak fool, echoing his father's abuse, and finally got the bolt forward, chambering a round.

Lifting the rifle once more, it felt even heavier with a few bullets inside, both physically and psychologically, but he was determined now to hit the target. Knowing he was going to get more unsteady with time, and desperate for this ordeal to be over, he squeezed off a round immediately. It ricocheted off a rock close to the one the bottle rested on. Missing the target he set his father off once more. With arms wide, head tilted back, his father appealed to God, asking why his son was so useless, and if, in being so useless, he had to be the only son he had.

Not my fault you've got lazy sperm, thought Tom. *That's right, I sneak into the den and read your mail, so what?*

But the thought, rather than bringing him a rebellious joy, instead made Tom sad, as he felt he was the natural product of the lazy sperm which had somehow still won the race to the egg in his mother's womb.

I'll always be a loser.

"Unless I make this shot," he whispered, hefting the rifle with renewed strength. His father saw he was trying again and quieted down, turning his eyes expectantly to the bottle, hands held together in pleading prayer as if the target were a holy altar and he was beseeching the Virgin Mother to give him a better son.

Tom experienced the same wavering of the iron sights for a moment, but then they drifted across his father. He found this gave him focus and a steely determination which lessened the movement of his aim. He settled the sights on the side of his father's head, and, for a moment, considered squeezing the trigger, though he decided against it easily and naturally.

However, in some type of subconscious granting of a wish he didn't know he'd long held and suppressed, his finger tightened without his volition. Tom watched in horrified slow motion as the rifle bucked like a bull, the butt slamming back like a battering ram, the resulting spike of pain making everything seem vibrant and all too real. The bullet left the barrel with an explosive flash and shot forward like a cast spear at a caveman's prey.

Then time sped up again with the whine of metal slicing the air, the bullet striking the glass bottle with a colourful explosion of shattering glass. Tom's father jumped back in shock, flinching as if he'd had the bottle balanced on his head. He stared incredulously at the point the bottle had been on the rock, the liquid it contained dripping down the rock's face like blood. Tom stared as well, unable to believe he'd made the shot.

But he knew he hadn't. It had been a fluke.

His father's praise rose up like a cry to heaven, but it fell on deaf ears, undeserved and unwanted by Tom. It did nothing to fill the void his lack of self-esteem had burrowed out of his heart long ago. He realised in that moment he could never please his father. But the revelation quickly evaporated, or was stored in a vault so deep, he couldn't access it again after that first revelation.

The words of his father touched only something superficial, a layer of his skin that was thin and fragile, the praise sinking in deep enough to mask the hurt he felt at his core. It was enough, for now, to soothe those ancient wounds, probably passed on to him by his father and his DNA.

We're all just a product of our DNA, thought Tom. This idea resonated with him, gave him an excuse for why he was like this, provided a mantra for life he would carry for a long time. It was a purpose, or the shadow of one. He saw it mirrored in his father as he ran up to his son, gave him a long-sought, rarely-given hug.

Tom looked into his father's eyes, saw his own reflection there, a little touch of the gold fever passed in that transference of light. It was something which was not love, but which masqueraded as love so well that Tom took it on board, let it cover him.

In that moment, he wanted nothing more than to see the yeti's head explode just like that bottle. It was either that, or to shoot his father in the head and bring this journey to its conclusion before they all had to suffer even more.

He couldn't bring himself to do that. Not consciously at least. But somehow he knew with certain conviction the only way this was going to end was in death.

3

"Now you're a crack shot," Tom's father said in a boastful tone which made it sound like he'd imparted all his skill and knowhow on his son in the field of weapons, "it's time to learn how to kill."

Tom baulked at the word *kill*, trepidatious at what his father had in store for him. He knew it would be nothing good, some new trial with a dubious moral lesson, his father floundering around in his attempt to make a man of his son.

He had no role model of his own, thought Tom. *Grandfather was a bastard who never loved him, tried to live vicariously through his son. Was that what made my father chase wealth? Are we all just trying to prove to our unloving fathers we're worth something?*

There was no repeat of the shot which broke the bottle, no second target placed to prove it was more than the fluke it was. His father was keen to move on, claiming the victory without consolidating his position.

It's always the same with him. If we find so much as something resembling a yeti footprint up there in the snow, he'll claim the prize already taken, no need for further action, and go home, a job well done, a story to tell.

Tom rolled his eyes, already suffering in the future.

A story I'll have to listen to, over and over, knowing half, if not more, of it is lies.

"Yes, any boy of thirteen can fire a rifle accurately," said his father, which made Tom fidget.

God, he doesn't even know how old I am.

"But a real man," continued his father, "knows how to kill an animal."

The hairs on the back of Tom's neck stood up, aware by the grandiose tone, the way his father spread his arms wide as if orating to a vast crowd, that the lesson was going to be a practical one in the worst sort of way, something approaching a spectacle which would burn itself into Tom's psyche.

"It's one thing to shoot a bottle," said his father. "Quite another to shoot for the heart, take a life. You must know where to shoot, and the consequences of the shot you take."

This, at least, made sense to Tom, but he didn't like where this was going, not at all. His father led him between some rundown buildings with low fences, shaking the Lord Kitchener rifle in the air like a bandmaster leading a marching band. He even hummed a jaunty tune from the old country, a militaristic one which gave him the air of a pathetic clown playing at soldiers. Tom followed along sadly, fiddling with the clip of .303 ammunition in his pocket, knowing he was going to be asked to do something dreadful.

Like shoot a yeti, a creature so rare barely anyone has seen it. A creature, if it exists, is surely endangered. But it was one he would have to help his father kill if he held on to any hope of ever getting his inheritance.

So that's it, thought Tom, disappointed with himself. *That's why I'm really playing along with this gross charade. It all comes down to money.*

And it was money that was making the difference right now as his father haggled loudly with a local farmer. It wasn't a friendly exchange, but one dominated by his father's overblown personality, the farmer being crushed under the weight of words being spat at him, loudly and slowly. Tom knew the man didn't understand any of it—he was making do with hand gestures himself, pointing at the money and holding up fingers. Unhappy with the price, Tom's father stuck the rifle in the man's chest.

God, thought Tom, *he's the richest man for hundreds of miles, and still he's trying to rob this poor peasant.*

But his father wasn't trying to rob the man. He was willing to pay, just not too much. He wanted to show who was boss. The farmer took less than his original price, dropping his fingers one by one until the rifle was lowered. Angrily, the farmer jerked his head off to one side, indicating where their merchandise was located. Tom followed behind his father, dreading what came next.

In the field was a yak. Tom's heart dropped. He knew what was coming before his father said it.

"You're going to kill this yak, and it's going to make you a man," he said.

No, it's not, it's just going to make me into whatever you are, thought Tom, touching the tip of each bullet in his pocket in turn, counting down the lives which were in his power—one, the yak, two, his father, three, the farmer, four, himself. The fifth would be left over for some other idiot to pick up this dead man's rifle, continue the dreadful cycle.

"The yeti is a big mammal, with lots of flesh around the chest, and a body covered in thick hair, just like this yak," explained his father, like any of this made sense. He patted the poor beast on its shoulder, which grunted as if in assent. His father beamed a smile at his son. "It's a perfect teaching tool."

Tom nodded dumbly.

"You'll notice I picked the one with white hair," said his father, stroking the lank strands of long fur. "I had to pay extra for that." He looked proud for a moment, pleased with himself and his wealth, but, as always, Tom watched his thoughts turn dark, his face contorting into a contemptuous sneer. "Greedy bloody locals."

"What do you care? You could buy every yak in this village and you'd not even notice," Tom found himself saying automatically, a long-held thought accidentally forcing its way through his lips.

"What did you say?"

Tom found the rifle pointed at him, but he knew it wasn't loaded. He held the bullets, the real power. He took a deep breath, puffing out his chest to pretend like he was something he wasn't.

"I said your factories make you enough money while we're talking to buy a hundred yaks."

His father's face went beet red, his whole body shaking with rage. "Give me the bullets," he said, his tone low and lethal, much scarier than the most explosive outburst.

Tom swallowed hard, reached into his pocket, pulled out the clip of five bullets. He held them out palm upwards, like an offering, knowing he was doomed, his father's eyes boring into his own.

This must be how all of father's prey felt, looking down the barrel of the gun, their death looming.

A trickle of pee ran down Tom's leg, hot like blood.

His father's face twisted in disgust, but at least the red drained from it, turning instead the colour of the snow-capped mountains, which watched in silent judgement. In that moment, Tom knew his father's approval was another such mountain, one he could never climb, but one he had to at least attempt in order to prove himself. He looked past his father and saw a string of climbers heading out on the hike to the Everest base camp.

I just wish it could be done peacefully. Instead, it has to be bought in blood, proven with killing.

He closed his fingers around the bullets, pulled them back.

"No," said Tom. "Give me the rifle."

He said it with such conviction, his father, who, at the end of the day, had no stomach for confrontations with real opposition, handed over the rifle without further fuss. Tom loaded the clip with a newfound confidence, stepped past his father and up to the yak.

It was a peaceful, placid beast, chewing cud slowly and methodically. Here was a creature with different needs than his own, living its life in a different lane, without the pressures Tom felt building in the base of his brain, stabbing at some primordial part of him which went back to the hunter gatherers, or even further, to the reptiles who were their distant ancestors and knew nothing but a bloody-minded focus on a game of predator and prey.

"I'm sorry," Tom said to the yak. He heard his father scoff at this, but he ignored him, looked deep into the eyes of the creature—they were shining black marbles. It stared back at him with dumb intelligence. Reaching out to touch its lank fur, yellowed and dank from a life in the mountain ranges, he felt a little shock of static electricity, as if the animal knew its death was coming and it was passing its vital essence to the one who held its life in their hands. The rifle felt heavier than ever. Tom decided the longer he delayed, the heavier it would get. He spun on the spot, started pacing out the hundred paces.

"No," said his father, gathering back his authority like a bundle of rags he had dropped on the ground. "No need to take the shot from a distance. You've proven you can hit a target. This part is about showing you have the will to follow through with it." He took a handkerchief out of his pocket, wiped his mouth, an excited gesture, anticipating the blood sport to come.

Tom glared at his father, his hatred plain. They were both well aware that at a hundred paces there was a chance he'd miss, probably a more than likely chance, and the boy would be spared the brutal lesson of having killed something. They also both knew he might maim the creature. That would turn this into a farce. What Tom wasn't sure of is if his father would make him shoot more and more bullets until the creature was dead.

But he wouldn't need so many, just one, straight through the heart. His father walked up to the yak, pointed out the exact spot on the creature's side. The yak kept chewing as if a death sentence hadn't been placed upon it, its life measured in mere minutes or seconds.

Tom approached, the rifle's barrel lowered, its weight far too much for him now. But his father grabbed the barrel, jammed it into the spot he'd pointed at. The yak stiffened, turned its head and looked right at Tom as if appealing its case. Tom wasn't the judge here, though he was the executioner.

"I can't do it," he mumbled.

"What's that?" his father said. His voice was like gravel being ground underfoot.

"I said I can't do it."

His father's tone lightened—his voice almost a singsong. "Do you love me, son?"

"Yes," said Tom. The lie came quickly and smoothly, made easy by long repetition.

"Then do it for me." His father attempted to smile, but it manifested as a dark grimace, teeth clenched, face muscles straining tight. "Do it for your old dad."

Still, Tom couldn't pull the trigger. There was a long pause, Tom's father holding his trump card, not wanting to play it, but willing to do so if the unbearable weight of silence proved futile. When Tom didn't succumb, he pulled it out.

"Do you want your inheritance, son?" his father asked.

Tom didn't answer. He hesitated long enough to prove to himself and his father that the answer wasn't automatic, then he pulled the trigger and the rifle spoke for him.

4

Tom's father sold the yak's meat for a profit on what he paid for the beast, which proved he could make money anywhere, doing anything. For all his faults, he was a self-made man and could talk anyone into anything.

Don't I know it, thought Tom, feeling the yak's death weighing upon his shoulders. Really it was just his heavy hiking pack. Even though his father hired a big team of local Nepalese Sherpas to haul most of their supplies, he said it was character building for Tom to carry his fair share, a good lesson in life. It must have been one of those 'do as I say, not as I do,' type things as his father didn't carry more than the Lee-Enfield rifle, a water bottle, and a stout hiking stick. Tom had watched him whittle the stick on the long cold nights they'd spent in their tent, waiting out bad weather, and even carve an intricate family crest into it, a total invention of the man's vanity and delusion. Tom had smiled and nodded mutely at the time he was shown this fabricated coat of arms, not wanting to say anything in case his father guessed he thought it pathetic. Now his father used this stick to rudely prod the Sherpas he thought were going too slow, fifty kilograms or more of supplies perched on their bent backs as they navigated the sharp rocks of the foothills.

Tom marvelled at these mountain men, their strength and resilience, and the way they not only abstained from complaining, but even joked and smiled a lot. To them the harsh conditions and his father's boorishness were part of the trade they plied, guiding rich Westerners through their homeland for a fee.

I suspect they put up with him in the hopes of a fat tip, Tom thought cynically. *Well, they're in for a rude shock. If they get a tip at all, it won't be a big one. Even that grudging pittance will be handed over only so they can't complain and my father looks magnanimous, the cheap bastard.*

Tom trudged on a few more steps, his boots slipping on the loose scree of rocks. A nearby Sherpa, despite his heavy load, reached out to steady him.

Perhaps I can spare them a bit of the cash I've got on me.

He frowned in concentration, shook his head. The Sherpa took it as a sign his assistance wasn't required and moved on.

No, I need that money for myself in case something happens to the old man. I have to get out of here somehow if he falls down a ravine or off a cliff. God, what a thought.

A cloud passed overhead, casting a shadow across his face. He started nodding without realising he was agreeing with a plan brewing in the dark spaces of his subconscious mind.

Yes, what a thought.

***

Another night, all too cold despite their gear, followed by yet another morning, breaking crisp and clear. It was a blessed relief to be able to emerge from the tent, go sit by the fire made by the Sherpas—up and busy before first light—and escape his father's close company. It afflicted Tom worse than the freezing temperatures or the depressing darkness of night.

The dawn sun struck the icy face of the mountain like a mirror, brilliant beams of light shooting in every direction like from a disco ball. Tom pulled out some sunglasses, perched them on his face. His father, grunting and coughing as he took a steaming piss nearby, turned to look at his son, huffed. He gave his cock a hearty shake and put it away, walked over to Tom. With no warning, he slapped the sunglasses from his son's face. Tom recoiled—the piss had frozen on his father's gloves and the blow stung. The urine quickly thawed beneath his nostrils.

He's trying to rub my face in it, prove he's still in charge, thought Tom as he went down on hands and knees to fetch up the sunglasses, but couldn't find where they'd gone.

"I don't want you wearing that crap. Ruins your depth perception," said his father, taking a mug of coffee from a waiting Sherpa. "You'll never see a yeti, white hair on white snow, with those sissy sunglasses on."

The Nepalese man glared at him but his father was too caught up in his spiel and his own sense of entitlement to notice. He didn't even thank the man, who retreated, blending into the background like the liveried servant his father took him for. He reappeared as if by magic, standing above Tom.

Tom looked up. The Sherpa held out the sunglasses, a broad beam slicing his face in half, crinkling the leathery skin into a thousand creases. Tom saw a tale told in those wrinkles—happiness and hardship, a life well-spent.

"Thank you," said Tom, taking the sunglasses and putting them back on. His father didn't seem to notice or care. He'd asserted his dominance, taught some obtuse lesson in yeti hunting to prove his wisdom and experience, and wasn't much concerned with the results, only appearances.

The Sherpa winked at Tom, took out a pair of his own sunglasses. They were cool wraparounds, the single, wide lens highly reflective in rainbow colours like an oil slick.

"I like your glasses," said Tom, getting up and sitting back down on his camp chair.

"Don't be talking to the help," said his father.

"They're people too."

His father grunted, doubtful of this. "If you show too much appreciation, they'll be asking for more money before you know it."

Tom stared into the flickering flames of the fire, the smoke rising up like a barrier between him and his father. "Someone must have shown you a hell of a lot of appreciation at some point then."

His father threw his mug of coffee down, the brown liquid staining the snow like dark blood, marking a primal challenge witnessed by primordial gods. A strangled cry tore from his throat as he leapt over the fire at his son, emerging through the smoke like an avatar of death, the black wisps twisting around his bestial features, contorted with rage.

Tom tried to duck away, but this only resulted in him falling backwards in his camp chair. His father landed on him, his weight snapping the chair legs. Tom writhed, shocked by the assault and not roused to anger himself, only confusion. He couldn't match his father's ferocity as the older man shook him violently. He bawled something incoherent in Tom's face. Although Tom couldn't understand him he could guess at the content. His mind filled in the blanks, summarised the bellicose barking as, "You're useless. You don't care about me. You don't care about the yeti. And unless you straighten up and fly right, you'll not see another penny from me."

The imagined words stung, in that they touched a lot of open sores in Tom's soul. Even the blows his father landed, taking up a broken chair leg and thrashing him like a rebellious slave, hurt less than those words, not so much spoken by his father, as interpreted by Tom, said in his own brain, revealing his faults, his weaknesses, and what he sought to prove to himself.

The Sherpas took hold of his father by the arms, dragged him off Tom. This sent the old man into even more of a blind rage. He struck out at the Nepalese men with the chair leg, who danced nimbly back from him, none of the blows landing. In his fury, Tom's father chased after them, clumsily stepping in the fire. He cursed in a long string of creative invective, most of it directed towards the Sherpas, stomping his singed boot in the snow. This seemed to cool him down a little, vented some spleen. He slowed, turning in a three sixty, the chair leg held out like a dagger to keep them all at bay.

Tom got up, stood with the Sherpas, joining them in a circle, surrounding his father and looking in on him in mute disapproval.

"What are you looking at?" shouted his father. "You bunch of useless mountain goats. Don't you know who I am? Don't you know how much I'm worth?"

The Sherpas didn't reply.

"I could buy and sell the lot of you like the stinking masses of yak meat you are."

This set the local men to muttering. The one with the sunglasses said something to them. They all looked at each other. Some shrugged, went back to their work, packing up the camp. Others shrugged also, but downed whatever tools or loads they were holding, abandoning them in the snow, started walking back down the lower slopes of the mountain carrying only what they had on their backs.

"What's going on?" asked Tom's father, lowering the chair leg. "Where are they going?"

"They're going home," the Sherpa with the sunglasses said in English.

"Home?" his father said in disbelief. He turned and marched a few steps down the slope in the crunchy snow, waving his arms above his head. "Hey! Hey you, come back. Don't you want to get paid?"

"They don't work for you anymore, Mister Tennyson," said the Sherpa.

"But we had a deal. Money talks, right? And when I speak, the world listens. You got that, you ignorant pile of yak dung?"

"Not everything is for sale." The Sherpa said it so plainly, with such conviction, that the wisdom of it resonated strongly, made Tom's father's statement as to the ways of the world sound false and hollow, a cheap replica only idiots would buy.

Tom smiled at this, pleased to have such a world view challenged, something he never experienced back home, everyone lining up for a piece of his father's fortune.

Even myself, he thought. *God, what am I doing here?*

"Who's going to carry all this stuff?" said his father, his whole body deflating, shoulders sagging under the weight of the consequences of his own loss of control.

"We'll carry what we can," said the Sherpa.

"And the rest?"

"You'll just have to make do with less."

Tom's father shook his head, unsatisfied with this conclusion, not wanting the world to work this way. "No, the lot of you are just going to have to carry more each."

The Sherpa sighed, looked at the men who had left, dwindling black spots against the snow, as if contemplating joining them, or perhaps in annoyance at the predicament they had put him in. Then he smiled, as if the whole thing had really been a blessing.

"I can shoulder more, but you must pay more," he said, matter-of-factly, nodding once in total confidence.

"And if I don't?" asked Tom's father.

"We leave you here to die on this mountain."

"You're saving on the ones who left. Just give these men the pay of the others, for their loyalty," said Tom.

His father swivelled slowly towards him, as if not believing he had the nerve to speak during a negotiation involving money. He stared Tom down, but Tom hid behind the sunglasses, managed to weather it. His father eventually looked away.

"You'll never get anywhere in life unless you learn to strike a bargain," he said to Tom, reverting back to his tried and true ways, that of the businessman. He smiled like a used car salesman at the Sherpas.

"I'll pay you half of those men's pay on top of your own if you carry their full loads," he said.

"Full loads, full pay," countered the Sherpa.

Tom's father looked around, as if surveying what was in the packs, doing an inventory he had left to other men to handle, for a fee. Tom knew it was all for show.

"We can lose a few things, especially as we don't need to feed those useless mules anymore," said his father, jerking a thumb over his shoulder at the retreating figures.

Tom pinched his nose.

He's totally clueless he's calling these men mules too.

He shook his head in self-contradiction.

No, he knows exactly what he's doing, devaluing them so as to drive the price down. And while it might work, it's pathetic. Why does he always have to be on top?

Tom thought about his father physically standing over him, thrashing him with that chair leg.

It won't always be the way though. One day I'll be stronger than him. Then he'll see.

"Half on top if you carry half again what you're presently carrying," said his father, as if nothing could be fairer. He smiled magnanimously, taking the glove off his right hand. He spat into the palm and extended it to the English-speaking Sherpa.

The man thought for a moment, looked around at his companions in silent communion. He turned back, nodded. Mirroring the gesture of Tom's father, they shook hands on the deal and the Sherpas got back to work, packing up the camp.

"Looks like they won't be leaving us to die out here after all," his father said to Tom conspiratorially, as if they were on the same side against the Sherpas, their relationship not strained at all by the beating Tom had taken. The shock having passed, he was feeling the welts swell up on his skin and chafe painfully against his heavy clothing.

"Do you have to rub everyone the wrong way?" he said to his father, who just gave him a look of total surprise, as if he had no clue what he was talking about.

"It's just business," was his reply.

"Everything is just business to you," Tom said under his breath.

His father tossed the broken chair leg away, kicked the shattered remains of the rest which lay in the snow, as if he had no clue how such a thing had happened. He went back to bossing around the Sherpas, who were packing everything the wrong way.

In this life, as long as he's around, there is the right way, the wrong way, and the Mister fucking Tennyson way.

Tom vowed to himself that if he was rich—and he was banking on that future—he'd do it different, treat people better. He just hoped the money itself didn't change him. For a moment, he looked down the slope at the retreating Sherpas, and wondered himself if they didn't have the right of it. Tom shook his head, sighed, and went to pack up his self-respect with the rest.

5

The English-speaking Sherpa sidled up to Tom, showing no signs of strain from the additional weight he carried and the steepness of the slope.

"It was very brave of you to stand up to my father like that," said Tom, stumbling and sliding in the crunchy snow.

"And cowardly of your father to beat you," the Sherpa said evenly, taking one step at a time, slow and methodical.

"He's not so bad."

Why am I defending him? thought Tom. But he couldn't help it. It was a family thing, and perhaps a cultural thing.

"My own father was strict too," said the Sherpa. "Not my birth father, but my Sherpa father. He knew, like your father knows, you have to be tough to survive."

"Here in the mountains?"

"The whole world is mountains. People in the West think things are easy because the land there is flat. It's an illusion." He shook his head sadly. "No, you have it harder. You do not have Chomolungma to teach you."

"Chomolungma?"

"It is the Tibetan word for the mountain." The Sherpa pointed at the snow, then up at the peak reverently, face serene. "In English, Holy Mother. It nurtures us, makes us strong."

"Tibetan? Not Nepalese?"

"I'm from Tibet, where I learned English from the monks. Afterwards my family sent me to live with the Sherpa people to learn their ways. My family was very poor. Here it is possible to survive, make money from Westerners who come to climb the mountain."

The Sherpa pointed off into the distance, further up the peak but on another face, where a team was climbing, white men with Sherpa guides, tied together with ropes.

"Is that why you put up with my father?" asked Tom.

"It's why you put up with him, no?"

Tom made a face. The Sherpa laughed.

"It is no judgement," he said. "We all get what we want out of life."

"And what do you want?" asked Tom.

"To be here on the mountain, climbing."

"And when you get to the top?"

"You come back down again. Rest. Climb again."

"I think in the West we prefer to stay on top, otherwise, what's the point of climbing?"

"The point of climbing is climbing. No man can stay on top forever. The mountain teaches us that. To live at such heights is death. I see it consuming your father."

"Sometimes he does act like he's starved of oxygen."

They both laughed, but Tom cast a cautious glance up the line of Sherpas, his father near the front, pretending to lead.

"He's going to get himself killed," said Tom.

"It's our job to make sure he doesn't," said the Sherpa.

"Because if he does he can't pay you."

"Yes, and if he goes home, says he had a great time, got everything he wanted from this climb, others will come, and my people will thrive."

"But he doesn't care about the climbing, only the yeti."

"The yeti and the climbing are one."

"What?"

"It's always been the way. The mountain, it scares people with its size, with its covering of deadly snow and ice, ready to crush the unwary man. Fear is what draws people to it. They seek to test themselves against its awesome power. The same goes for the yeti. Both are forces of nature, something man wishes to overcome. But while man can stand astride a mountain, they cannot conquer the yeti."

"They can kill it," said Tom, pointing at his father, at the rifle slung across his shoulders.

"The yeti is the one who kills, not man."

"And yet you persist on this mission, taking us to our doom."

The Sherpa laughed. "No doom. We will find no yeti, because the yeti does not wish to be found. Some footprints, yes, but no yeti. If we see it, it sees us, it will flee."

"But you said it kills."

"If it has to. It is not a blood hungry monster like people think, just a living creature, same as you and I. It will avoid us and only attack if cornered."

"And if we corner it?"

The Sherpa pointed up at a deadly serac, far ahead, the large block of ice overhanging their route like a sword of Damocles. “It lets the mountain do the killing. But I won’t let that happen to you.”

“You’ll protect my father as well, save him from the mountain?”

The Sherpa nodded his head. “He’s a fool, but right in this—money makes the world go around. I’m no hypocrite. As I said, my family sent me here to survive. This is how we survive, taking naïve Westerners up into the snow and ice, where the air is thin, in pursuit of the yeti.”

Tom’s eyes went wide. “You’ve done this with others? My father thinks he’s the only yeti hunter.”

“No. Many have come before. The first white man who climbed the mount, Edmund Hillary, he came for the yeti as much as for the summit.”

“What did they find?”

“The footprints his Sherpa guide showed him. It was enough, then the passion was sated, and he could be redirected towards the peak. A goal secondary to the myth became a famous achievement.”

“His guide sounds like a wise man.”

“He was a great mountaineer, the best. Tenzing Norgay. I am named after him.”

“Your name is Tenzing?”

Tenzing flashed his brilliant smile. “Yes, it is quite a common Sherpa name. There is another even on this trek. Norgay became a national hero, very famous.”

“Edmund Hillary is famous back home, but not so much Tenzing.”

The Sherpa scoffed. "It is always the way with the white man, taking all the credit."

"My father wants the credit of being the man who killed the yeti."

"He'll be lucky to even see it."

Tom rubbed his fingers together, a universal sign. "If he doesn't find the yeti, he'll not pay you."

"He'll pay. They see the footprint and they go weak in the knees."

"Not my father. That alone will not satisfy him. He's a stubborn man."

"All white men are stubborn, like the yak."

"But not nearly as peaceable."

"No, that they are not. They are restless, like the yeti, as are the Sherpas, always hiking. We live to hike."

The Sherpa smiled in such a way—with his eyes, showing no teeth—that Tom knew the conversation was over. The Sherpa wanted to go back to enjoying his trek for its own sake, taking one methodical step after the other and looking at the gorgeous scenery.

Tom did the same, but while the mountains were spectacular all around, their beauty now felt like a thin veneer, like a stage backdrop, hiding something sinister, a twist in the play Tom wasn't expecting.

Tenzing thinks the yeti is real. He certainly seems confident we'll find footprints, if not the yeti itself. But if there are footprints, something must have made them. I thought this whole thing a wild goose chase, the real danger being the mountain and my father's megalomania. I had just been starting to get over the tall tales, face the reality. Now it seems there is a monster out there after all.

He stopped to catch his breath, the going hard and his leg muscles aching.

And my father won't give up until he's found it, or died trying—if not on this trip, then the next or the one after that. He'll drag me along each time, my own death probably a statistical inevitability, given the lethality of Everest itself.

Tom looked up at the serac again, the block of ice looming, waiting to fall and crush them, a type of Russian roulette all climbers played as they walked beneath its ominous bulk.

We're playing with bad odds, and the house always wins.

6

The next day broke bright and clear, the view breathtaking as they exited their tents on the snowy ledge. But this awe-inspiring view wasn't one directed outwards, at the surrounding mountain peaks, with their glistening ice and snow, but inwards and down, at the ground, where there was something in the thick snow on the slopes of Mount Everest.

It was a footprint.

The Sherpas gathered around it, talking excitedly in their own language, each of them trying to lean in close, pointing out the features they saw, as well as the great size of the thing. Tom tried to get in for a look, jumping up and down to see over their hunched bodies.

"Get back, you mongrels," said his father, shoving them aside with the handle of his ice pick. They voiced their discontent at this, buzzing like a hive of angry bees, but let him through. Tom darted in behind in his wake. His father threw his arm over his shoulder in a rare fatherly gesture, drew him in close so their heads were touching.

"Blimey, son, will you look at that," he whispered conspiratorially, trying to exclude the Sherpas from this special moment.

This is what he paid for, after all, thought Tom.

The Sherpas started singing a chant, stomping their feet to the beat. Tom's father stood up straight, held the pick by its handle, its blade flashing like a violent threat in the sunlight. "You'll ruin the trace with your damn jumping about. I said get back, God damn you."

But the Sherpas were just as fixated on the footprint as his father and ignored him.

"There's another one," said Tom, pointing. "And even more over there." Up over some ice the tracks disappeared, but they started again in the thick snow beyond.

"Bloody hell, you're right. That's a good eye, boy," said his father. Tom beamed a smile, his whole face lighting up with the praise. They left the Sherpas to the first footprint, went and inspected the string of them which led further up the mountain.

"Look at the size of the thing," said his father, laying his pick down next to it for scale and whistling, impressed. "It must be twenty inches long." He got out his camera, a very expensive Kodak model, and took pictures, smiled a contented smile Tom rarely saw. For a moment he dared to dream this would be enough for his father, that they could now go home, or at least just climb the mountain, accomplish something which wasn't mad. He looked up at the peak, still high above.

Well, less mad.

"Just like Hillary," said his father, shaking the camera. "He got the same photo, with his pick, but our footprints are bigger, see?"

"Oh, so you know about Edmund Hillary looking for the yeti?"

"Of course I know about that. Why do you think we're here?"

"You never told me."

His father actually looked abashed, which shocked Tom.

"I wanted you to think I was the first, that it was my idea," he said, which shocked Tom even further, nearly blew him over to see a chink in his father's armour for once. It was a moment of vulnerability which quickly passed, the braggadocio returning in spades to fill that small weak spot.

"This is just about the last mistake that yeti ever made," said his father, inspecting each of the tracks in turn, following their line for a few dozen yards. He shielded his eyes against the sun. "They lead up towards the serac there and beyond. By gum, we've got him now."

Tom breathed out, his breath misting in the frigid air, the mountainside cold despite the sun. He had a bad feeling about this and said so to his father.

"Your yellow streak is showing," was the reply, which hurt Tom and deflated him all the more for the recent compliment he'd received about his good eye.

"You don't think it's a bit… convenient that the tracks were left here?" Tom rubbed the back of his neck nervously. "I mean, standing on this spot we've a prime view down the mountain, could see anyone coming up this route."

"We took this route precisely because it's not used much, far away from the one the *climbers* take." His father said the word climbers with a sneer.

"It could be a trap, a setup."

"Do you really think someone would bother to come up here, fake these tracks, just to do God knows what, ambush us? What a bunch of nonsense."

"I'm talking about the yeti."

"You've some imagination, boy, I'll give you that."

"You said it was cunning."

"Yes, but—"

"Yes, but what? What exactly do you think it capable of?" Tom asked.

"Not something like this. I meant it can hide behind a rock maybe, jump out at you."

"I think it is hiding, and these tracks aren't meant to lead us to it."

"What are they then?"

Tom looked down the footprints. They were truly humungous, and filled him with dread. "I think it's a warning."

"Not bloody likely. The yeti is on the run."

"You see these tracks," said Tom. He was shouting, his voice rising hysterically. "What do you think could have made them? Something we can hunt and kill? It's huge. It's a wild monster. We'll not leave this mountain alive."

"Son," said his father calmly, sounding far too reasonable to Tom's ears. "I've travelled the world. I've hunted tigers in India, hippos in Africa, wild boar in Australia, and much more besides. There isn't a creature alive I fear, not with this in my hand." He unslung the rifle, hefted it, aimed down at one of the footprints, pretended to line up a shot, fire into them. "Who cares if it's big? Who cares if it's ferocious? You think the elephants I've slain were small, the lions I tracked were timid?"

"The yeti is like a big ape, though, maybe with intelligence approaching that of a man. Have you ever hunted a man?" asked Tom, trying to snap him back to reality.

"Yes," his father said, fixing Tom with a hard stare. "I have."

In that moment, Tom feared for his own life, because he finally saw the depth to which his father had sunk, the depravity his lust for the hunt had driven him to. The gaze wasn't one of a man, but of an apex predator—cold, black, and blank.

Perhaps that is the true gaze of man, the true primal nature of what we are, thought Tom. He expected to feel fear at this, but instead he felt sad, because it seemed to him that he was staring at his future self, a genetic legacy waiting for him if he continued down this path towards damnation.

The yeti won't be the end of this. There is no end to this, except death. And if I let myself catch the same savage fever my father has, I'll be doomed too.

"I want to go home," he said simply.

His father pointed the rifle at him. "You'll go home when I say we can go home."

A shadow passed in front of Tom, blotting out the sun, shielding him from his father.

It was Tenzing.

"Time to push for the summit, right, Mister Tennyson?" he said, ignoring the loaded rifle which was now pointed at his chest.

Tom's father sidestepped, tried to confront his son again. Tenzing sidestepped as well, continuing to protect Tom. But Tom didn't want to be protected, he wanted to face his father, to oppose him, show that he stood for something different. He sorely missed the rifle from his hand. Now he understood why his father had not brought along two rifles. It meant he always had the power, only relinquishing it when he wanted, both aspects designed to teach his son a single brutal lesson—might makes right.

It is to turn me into him. But that's not what I want.

Even as he thought this, he knew there was no escape. Not from his father, not from this mountain, and certainly not from his fate.

But I can wield that fate, make it my own. I can take back my power.

"No," said Tom, putting a hand on Tenzing's shoulder and easing him aside. He spoke into the emotionless face of his father, seeing a dark mirror of his own soul. "We go after the yeti."

7

The climbing got more physically challenging all the time, up steep slopes of thick snow, traversing ice, scaling cliffs. Panting hard with exertion, Tom realised he'd been mad to come on such an advanced expedition.

Like I had a choice, he thought grimly, glaring daggers into his father's back. He still wanted to go home, but was well aware the only way back was forward. Only once they confronted the yeti could they quit.

The mood of the Sherpas had changed—Tom's father a different beast than all the other rich Westerners they'd dealt with.

They must think he's mad.

Tom turned around to look at Tenzing, climbing behind, whose unsmiling face was as blank and emotionless as the banks of flat, white snow underfoot.

They think I'm mad too now. I've crossed over to the other side.

This thought made him sad. He'd much prefer to be with these stoic, happy people than siding with his father. But birth, race, class and more placed him with the stubborn old fool instead of these wise mountain-folk.

If we bag the yeti maybe I'll prove myself to be their equal.

He shook his head, stopped to lean on his knee, catch his breath.

No, that would take me further away. It's my father who wants the yeti. These men would just as well leave it alone.

His breathing became even more laboured, ragged gasps provoked by anxiety.

I feel trapped.

"Are you alright, Master Tom?" asked Tenzing, though he didn't stop, maintaining his own rhythm, feet rising and falling methodically. The other Sherpas passed too, the line of them looking like a conveyer belt on a factory floor, machine-like the way they hauled the supplies up this impossible terrain.

"The air is starting to get a bit thin," said Tom.

The back of Tenzing's head creased against his neck, nodding, though he said, "This is nothing. No need for oxygen yet."

"How do I continue?" asked Tom, not wanting to sound pathetic, but hearing the whine in his voice.

"Take one step at a time. Rest for a moment when you need to."

So Tom rested, tried to suck in deep breaths, replenish the oxygen in his blood, his lungs feeling like thin paper bags, inflating and deflating with a dry crinkling sound. Slowly he improved, finding reserves of strength were to be had with the most meagre of resources. He looked around at the terrain. While it was still beautiful, it was desolate, not made to support life.

Does the yeti really live all the way up here?

Tom knew this couldn't possibly be the case, but then why had the tracks led them up this high? There wasn't anything at this altitude to hunt.

Except man, of course.

He looked down at the footprints of his father and the Sherpas. Each was swallowed up in the much larger footprints of the yeti they followed. More than ever, Tom felt that not only he, but all of them were not equal to the task ahead. Sure, there was a whole team of men, and only one yeti.

But were those good enough odds?

***

"There are two of them," said Tom's father in astonishment, one hand on his hip, the other holding his head, boggled by the concept as he looked down at the two sets of yeti prints. "By God, there are *two* sets of tracks."

"This is a good place for a camp," announced Tenzing, ignoring him. The Sherpas were no longer interested in the tracks, no longer showed them any reverence and awe. They exhibited only numb exhaustion and silent fear. The possibility that there were two yetis seemed to drain them of the last of their energy. They dropped their heavy loads, and then themselves, into the thick snow with a single loud crunch at Tenzing's pronouncement. None made any move to start clearing a site for the tents. They looked like frozen corpses, a light drift of snow starting to fall which would eventually cover them, the world forgetting they ever existed.

The last in the line, having long ago fallen behind, Tom finally approached and then passed them. The faces of the men were grey like gravestones. He suspected he looked even worse.

Each laboured breath he took misted in the air, further obscuring the Sherpas' features until they blended into the snow, becoming vague silhouettes in the fading light at the end of the day. They resembled the dark rocks poking their tips above the snow. Tom navigated around them as he had so many inert obstacles on this gruelling march up the world's tallest mountain.

"Tom. Come here, boy," his father shouted over his shoulder. He'd not once looked back to check on his son, see how he'd been faring in the tough conditions, his eyes always fixed on the ground and the tracks, completely blind to all else.

Tom paused a few steps back from his father, his ice pick held limply in his hand. His father repeated his summons with more urgency. "Tom!"

His teeth grating at the sound of his own name, Tom gripped the handle of the ice pick a bit tighter, let the weight of the steel head swing slightly like a pendulum.

It would be so easy to plant this in the back of his head, end this.

He glanced at the Sherpas, checked they weren't watching. Tenzing seemed to be purposefully avoiding looking his way, craning his neck up to inspect the sky. Tom turned back to glare at his father. Despite the cold, sweat dripped off his forehead, into his eyes, making him blink rapidly. With his heart beating hard in his ears like a drum, he clenched his fist on the pick's grip so hard his whole arm shook. The tension built in his whole body until it hummed like a strung bell.

It reached a crescendo, until he thought he might snap. Instead, he pulled himself back from the edge, hearing the voice of his dead mother in his mind.

You don't have to be like him.

His clenched fist released. The pick hung loose from the cord looped around his wrist. He cast one more glance at the Sherpas, envying their anonymity, the way their father cared so little about them, for better or worse, and wished he could lie down with them, be one of them, if only for a moment. How he longed to let the snow cover his face, be forgotten.

"I said, come here, boy," shouted his father, so loud it drowned out any softer, kinder voice he might hear in his mind. His father made a summoning gesture with his arm without turning. Tom felt the leash connecting them tighten and he was dragged forward involuntarily.

He stumbled up beside his father, saw what he saw. It was a shock, even though he'd heard his father's pronouncement about there being two sets of tracks. But he didn't expect it to look like this. To Tom it had been an obvious deduction, a foregone conclusion that the second set of tracks would appear beside the first, running parallel, proof there was a pair of yetis, walking together side by side. Perhaps the first had gone to collect its mate, was leading them to safety, away from the humans.

Instead, the single set of tracks they'd been following proliferated into two, branching like an intersection in a road, one leading further up the mountain, the other angling down the slope, pointing back towards base camp.

"What do you make of that, boy?" said his father, shaking his head in disbelief, eyebrows raised speculatively.

"Maybe there had been two yetis all along, walking in each other's footprints," suggested Tom.

"That would be some neat trick, but would require a delicate touch I'm not sure the yeti is capable of."

"You don't know what the yeti is capable of." Tom said the words with sharp conviction, trying to break the ice of his father's resolve, make him see reason.

His father ignored him, continued with his own thoughts as if he was speaking to himself, Tom just a sounding board, not a person at all. "No, I've been watching the tracks like a hawk every step of the way. Even if they were careful there's no way I'd not notice."

"Your senses are that sharp, are they?"

Tom's father looked up at him, his eyes glassy, as if it was taking a moment for him to focus on his son, identify him.

I wonder if he's going snow blind?

"Like a hawk, boy. Did you not listen?" said his father with indignant conviction. "A hawk, I say," he added absently, returning to his close inspection of the tracks, bending double at the waist, his son once again forgotten.

Tom crouched down to ease the burning in his thighs, the aching in his calves, but also to have a closer look at the footprints. Both sets of tracks seemed to be identical in length, made not by two different sized yetis—no larger male and more diminutive female. Indeed, they were such a match they could possibly be made by the exact same creature.

"Tenzing," said Tom over his shoulder. "Come here." He almost accidentally added the word *boy* to the end of that sentence, but managed to pull himself up at the last.

God, I am *becoming him.*

"Master Tom?" inquired Tenzing, responding to the summons just as quickly as if he were the man holding the purse strings and not his father.

Perhaps one day I will be, thought Tom, giving those imaginary strings a little test tug with his hand, a gesture which Tenzing took to mean he should crouch down beside him, take a look at the tracks. The Sherpa spent a long while without speaking, both Tom and his father watching him, Tom the more patient of the two, his father rocking back and forth.

I'm sure he's thinking 'time is money,' or some other such nonsense, thought Tom.

"One yeti or two?" he asked the Sherpa after a while, his own patience having its limit.

"This is a single yeti," said Tenzing. He indicated one set of prints with his outstretched palm as if lifting a copy, then transferred and imprinted it in the snow where the second set branched off. "Same, same."

"How is that possible?" asked Tom's father brusquely, not satisfied with the answer.

"The yeti is an elusive creature. It is like a ghost. Here it has split itself in two. The yeti goes one way, its spirit the other."

"Damn it, man. It's a beast, not some supernatural entity."

"We're guests here, Father. It doesn't pay to disrespect the local beliefs," said Tom, also unsatisfied with the answer but not wanting to offend Tenzing.

The Sherpa stood up. "That is not a belief, just a guess. But one thing is clear. The yeti is offering you a choice. One path leads up the mountain, the other down."

"I'm not turning back now," said Tom's father, taking off his woollen cap and wringing it in his hands. "Bloody hell, we've come this far. I'm not going to be put off just because the yeti says go home."

"It's warning us," said Tom.

His father put his cap back onto his head, tugging it down like a soldier does their helmet before going into battle. "It's scared, is what it is. This is just some cheap ploy. I've seen it before. Head off in one direction, then carefully backtrack in your own steps, off you go another way. It's trying to throw us off."

"So, what do we do? Flip a coin?"

"You really think I'm going back that way?" His father pointed along the tracks heading down the mountain. "No, we go up."

Tenzing sucked his teeth, clicked his tongue, and then shook his head. "We cannot allow you to do that."

"Bloody mutiny is it now, eh?"

"We have trekked hard, carried your supplies up the Holy Mother's unforgiving flanks. For this, it is normal for us to seek to be paid for our labour, but we do not seek to make you pay with your life."

Tom's father started to unsling his rifle from his back. "Is that a threat?"

Tenzing held up a palm to forestall this. "It is a promise. If you persist in this madness, the yeti—or the mountain, which is its home and protector—will kill you."

"What about you though, eh? You and your mates going to slit my throat in the night, take off with my money?"

Tenzing looked genuinely hurt by this, his facial features sagging low.

"How could you suggest such a thing?" said Tom, outraged on the Sherpas' behalf.

Because it's what he himself would do in their place, he reflected darkly.

"You want to get paid, you want *any money at all*, then you pitch the damn tents, you fire up the stoves, and get my dinner ready," his father said to Tenzing. He pulled the rifle off his shoulder, shook it like a war spear. "In the morning, we go after the yeti."

8

In the morning the tracks were gone, covered by the snow which fell in the night, and with them, the final warning of the yeti. The choice had been revoked. Now all that remained was the threat, or promise, of inevitable death—either theirs or the yeti's.

Tom could tell the Sherpas were in no hurry to die. They were sluggish in their movements as they packed up the camp, all their joking and smiling gone, left behind somewhere further down the mountain. Their attitude now mirrored the bitter, desolate environment around them, icy and stone-faced.

The only one smiling was Tom's father, and it was the feral grin of a predator. Even with the tracks gone, he was confident in his direction, aiming for the peak which pointed upwards like a directing arrow, guiding them towards a final showdown with the terrible beast.

Tom wasn't keen on that impending moment, but he faced it with grim resolve. They'd left behind the world, far below them now, where his father's wealth cushioned him from reality and took the hard edges off life. Up here on Everest life was all hard edges, the jagged rocks of the mountain closing in like the chomping teeth of a monster, ready to cleave them in two, spill their guts, drink their blood.

He took a piss on the snow. It melted at the touch of the hot liquid, but then froze again, leaving little more than a stain—his blood would have a similar, temporary effect.

This mountain really can swallow us whole without a trace.

***

One moment the Sherpa was there, the next he was gone. It was like a magician's disappearing act, a trapdoor opening in the snowy ground and the man going down through it in a single motion. It was accompanied by a sluicing rumble of tumbling snow and ice beneath Tom's feet and a harrowing scream which sounded like an echo.

Tom blinked hard, felt a single thudding heartbeat—then something even more visibly dramatic happened. Another Sherpa was tugged violently from his feet as if by the hand of a giant. Tom's first terrified impression was that the yeti had got the drop on them, sneaking through the cloudy fog, naturally camouflaged with its white hair, and smashed the two men with its mighty, ham-sized fists. But Tom felt a tug at the rope tied to his harness. Tenzing— who was attached to the other end of it—darted forward in an attempt to save at least the second man, who skittered across the ice, cursing and wailing. A rope led from that Sherpa to the hole through which the first had disappeared—they were a roped-together team the same as Tenzing and Tom—and he was being dragged to the same fate as his mate.

Tenzing made a dive for the man. It was only at this point that Tom realised he was involved. The rope which tied him to Tenzing embroiled him in this life and death struggle. He threw himself down on his butt, tried to make himself into an anchor by wriggling into the icy snow.

It wasn't necessary. Nor was it any help.

Though Tenzing reached the man before he was dragged down the hole, grabbing him with an outstretched hand, the loads the men carried on their backs was their undoing. The first Sherpa who fell was too much of a weight on the other end, falling at great speed, and this ripped his mate from Tenzing's grasp.

It all happened in a few seconds. The second Sherpa was gone with a final shrieking scream, sucked down into the hole as if it were a vortex which led to another world. There was a moment of total stillness which followed, the whole party facing the hole in horrified silence, as if waiting to see if this hungry maw was satiated by the two it had already eaten, or if it wished to claim more blood and flesh for its frozen stomach.

Tenzing and Tom got up slowly, both stiff with shock, their bodies pumping adrenaline which made their skin sting. They shuffled towards the place where the snow became a little more blue than white, the ice walls of the shaft of the hole reflecting some light. They stood around the edge of the hole, looking down into it, as if their heads were bowed in a prayer for the fallen.

Tom nearly jumped out of his skin and fell down the hole as his father erupted like a long dormant volcano finally blowing its lid.

"You fucking idiot," he bellowed, stomping over to cuff Tenzing around the back of the head. The Sherpa took it uncomplainingly, only flinching slightly, his attention still on the hole. "You could have taken my son down that damn hole with you, pulling a stunt like that." Tom's father was shouting right in Tenzing's ear.

"He was trying to save a man's life," said Tom.

His father turned on him, shoving a trembling finger in his face. "You think any ten of these dirty bastards is worth my only son."

Tom sunk his heels into the snow. "Do you think *you're* worth your only son?"

"What's that supposed to mean?"

"It means I'm embarrassed by you. Two men just died and all you care about is yourself."

His father swelled up in rage, went to speak, stopped, spluttered out a held breath, deflating a little. He slapped a hand down on Tom's shoulder. "I only care about you."

Tom shook the hand off. "You only care about yourself and your legacy. That's all I am to you, a way for you to extend your life beyond death. I'm not a person, not a man. If you recognised any such thing you'd see two good, honest, hardworking human beings have lost their lives. Two *men*, with families to support, dead, helping you chase after a pipedream."

"It's no pipedream. You saw those tracks."

"My God, a person stomping about in special boots could make those tracks. You think Tenzing is a fool? You're wrong. You're the fool."

His father raised his hand to strike him, but the blow never landed. Instead, the old man let out a strangled cry as Tenzing lifted him by the scruff of his jacket, dragged him close to the edge of the hole. His father struggled in the strong man's grip, tried to plant his feet. Tenzing angled him forward so his centre of gravity was hanging over the abyss.

"You let me go, right now, you damn mongrel," said Tom's father. "Don't forget who's paying you."

Tenzing's face was an unmoving mask, the pleas falling on deaf ears. He leant forward more. The old man was dangling, feet kicking the inner wall of the hole.

"Wait," said Tom, "don't do that."

But Tenzing released his grip, let his father drop.

9

The fall was not a long one, quickly punctuated by a snapping sound of the rope. It had not broken, just taken the weight of Tom's father, whacking against the snow and ice as it went taught. Tom looked down into the hole. His father spun on the line, cursing colourfully and kicking the ice walls with the spikes of his crampons, trying to get a purchase. But he wasn't going anywhere, neither up nor down. On the other end of his rope was a big Sherpa, the teammate he'd been tied to during the climb. Taking some subtle cue from Tenzing, he'd dropped down like Tom had before, his purchase made sturdier by a makeshift snow anchor he carved out, around which he'd wound the rope and braced his weight.

Tom let out a breath he'd been holding. His father was safe—though why he cared so much he didn't know. It would have been a convenient end to this ordeal, almost inevitable really. No one would blame him, and he'd keep quiet about the role of the Sherpas. It was the easy option, but not to be. His father was alive, saved by the rope team system, unlike the two Sherpas, one of whom had been doomed by that which was meant to keep him safe, the other by the fickle fortunes of the mountain.

Tom could see their mangled and unmoving bodies through the hole, fifty yards or more down the rift in the ice, still tied together, as they would be forever now. Ice was already forming on their faces, the beginning of a natural process which would provide them with a frozen tomb, their bodies unrecoverable this high up the mountain.

"Let's get him up," Tom said to Tenzing, who broke into a smile—the first seen from the Sherpas in a while—and nodded. They all hauled at the rope, his father not making it easy on them, moving around too much, trying to get his own footing, but failing, totally reliant on them for his rescue.

More than once Tom thought about leaving him down there, as he was sure Tenzing had too. Finally, with much effort, they dragged him over the lip of the hole. Spluttering with barely contained fury, he got up, dusted the snow off his clothes.

"How dare you pull a stunt like that," he said. His face was red and quivering.

Tenzing smiled even wider, the pleasantness of it masking a grim resolve for personal dignity. "You told me not to forget who's paying me," he said to Tom's father, who nodded, bearing his teeth with a sneer.

"That's right, and if you think you're getting any type of tip at the end of this then you're—"

Tenzing grabbed him again, this time around the lapels of his jacket. He pulled him close and gave him a little shake to make him shut up. Tom watched as his father's trembling gaze turned from Tenzing to his own rope mate, who had conspicuously come up beside them, undoing the rope from his harness and tossing the end down the hole.

Tenzing shuffled Tom's father back towards the edge, and said, "And I'm telling you, don't forget who's keeping you alive."

***

After much frantic nodding of acknowledgement from Tom's father, as well as desperate promises of more pay, Tenzing dragged him away from the hole, dumping him unceremoniously on the hard snow. He had the good sense to lie there a while and keep his mouth shut as the Sherpas reorganised, taking inventory of the supplies and equipment they still had, and what had been lost down the hole.

When that was done they gathered around that icy rift in a solemn ring, sung dirges and said prayers, clapping their hands quietly. Tom and his father watched, feeling like the outsiders they were. Tom would have liked to join in, but he knew he'd be intruding—this was Sherpa business. And while he himself blamed his father for the deaths—they wouldn't be up here if not for his stupid yeti hunt—Tom got the sense the Sherpas didn't see it this way. The mountain had claimed those two men, as it often claimed a toll for their making a living from it. It was part of their way of life, an inevitable yet unfortunate consequence of their vocation.

Still, it didn't sit easy with Tom. He wished they could see sense, give it up, money be damned. But one glance at his father, perched beside him on an ice-covered rock, put a swift end to any notion of going home. There was a burning intensity to the old man's stare, directed at the Sherpas in general and Tenzing in particular.

He's been humiliated and wants to salvage his dignity.

Tom knew there was only one way that was going to happen—by hunting and killing the yeti, taking its head home as a trophy to hang on the wall.

And if his father couldn't have the yeti's head, Tom was sure he would settle for Tenzing's.

***

"Time to move on," said Tenzing, pointing towards the summit, making no mention of the yeti. Tom felt his father tense beside him. The old man was used to giving the orders. But Tenzing was clearly done mucking about. The Sherpas tied themselves together in a rope team which didn't include the two Westerners, who were left to pair up separately as a second team.

"But the boy's not strong enough to hold my weight if I fall," said Tom's father. "I want that big fellow, the one who caught me when you—"

Tenzing glared at him, daring him to continue, to accuse him. Tom knew if he did there would be a repeat of the whole incident, but with no one to break his fall this time.

Except me, and Father's right, I'm not strong enough to catch him, thought Tom. *I don't want that responsibility. I can't save him. My whole life he's been falling in slow motion. Maybe he has to hit the bottom, learn the hard way? But if he does is there any way to come back?*

He looked at his father. With the snow thick in his beard he looked even older than usual. His eyes were alight though, driven by rage and an enflamed ego.

What type of mad midlife crisis has brought you up this mountain? You're killing yourself doing this, you know that, right?

Tom felt a tug on the rope as his father turned and started trudging up the mountain in the wake of the Sherpas. He tried to resist, wanting to set his own pace, but his father took up the slack, pulled him along like a disobedient puppy.

And this time he's going to take me down with him.

10

They climbed towards the serac, its blue ice tucked into the sharp crevices between vertical bands of black rock. It was a daunting obstacle, looming over them like the wall of a great castle. This giant slab of frozen water stood sentinel over the path they would have to take, guarding the way to the summit. There was no other route anymore—the heavy snows had seen to that, making avalanches more likely back the way they had come, the descent perilous. Nor could they go around the serac, hemmed in by ridges which blocked their path and could only be scaled with the most advanced climbing techniques. This might be possible for the Sherpas but was beyond the skill of Tom and his father, mere amateur mountaineers.

Tom never felt more reliant on Tenzing and the other Sherpas than he did in that moment, and for all his bravado, all his money and power, his father was as helpless as he was. The two of them were no more than lost boys, being hauled up the world's tallest peak by the sheer will and skill of these sturdy mountain men.

Tom was well aware Tenzing was just trying to get them to the top now, hoping and praying that if he could place his father on the summit it would appease him, as it had all the others who had come before.

He doesn't know my father though.

But before they could tackle the summit they faced the greatest test—the serac. The only way past it was beneath, running the gauntlet, hoping their luck held. The rope-teams edged forward into the shadow of the overhang of ice. Everyone's eyes were upwards, watching the serac warily. Tom couldn't help but think there was another way—that they didn't have to face this terrible danger.

Do we really have any reason to believe the yeti has come this way? It could have doubled back, leaving the mountain to kill its pursuers. If it is as cunning as everyone professes, then surely that is the safest and most obvious option for the yeti. It's what I would do.

"But you're a coward," Tom said to himself, his knees shaking, and not just from the bitter cold. He looked up at the serac, imagined its immense weight falling on him, crushing him flat. He almost fainted, swooning on the spot. To his surprise his father doubled back to him, struggling through the thick snow with heavy, dragging steps.

"Time for the oxygen, boy," he said. "I'm starting to feel a bit woozy myself."

He took the equipment from his son's pack, rigged up the oxygen bottle and, with a gentleness Tom had not experienced from his father since his mother had died, placed the mask upon his face.

Tom took a few deep breaths, feeling better immediately, the oxygen spiking his system like a drug. After a few minutes his mind sparkled, the light of the sun seeming brighter, bouncing off the snow and ice in a brilliant rainbow display of refracted colours. In this heady rush of clarity, Tom looked once more at the serac. With a feeling of euphoria washing over him, he didn't feel so afraid anymore. The ice shelf would hold instead of crushing them all to death.

He smiled, his body relaxing, releasing tension which had knotted up his muscles. His joints limbered up, less constricted with cold, and his skin tingled with heat in a way which both stung painfully and yet was a relief. For a moment he didn't feel like he was in danger or that his life hung in the balance. He felt safe, his heart beating loudly in his ears like an encouraging drum.

Then his blood froze in his veins.

Directly beneath the centre of the serac, walking slowly and methodically a few hundred yards away, was something he'd not been expecting to see, had indeed been banking on never ever catching so much as a glimpse of. But yet here it was, plain as day.

The yeti.

For a moment, Tom was sure he was hallucinating. Too much oxygen inhaled too quickly had warped his brain. But he lifted a trembling finger, pointed at the vague shape, white fur blending into a background of white snow. His father twisted to see what he was indicating, made a strange barking sound in his shock of recognition. It quickly turned into a whoop of triumph. "Hoo roo," he shouted.

The sound of it echoed, far too loud to Tom's heightened senses. The yeti obviously heard it as well, as it turned on the spot. Tom saw the dark, leathery skin of its face and hands. The terrible visage of the monster twisted into a silent roar, its mouth wide in challenge or fear. Then the yeti took off, running away from them, beneath the serac, far more nimble than its great size would suggest it capable of.

"There it goes, by God," said Tom's father. He spent a few seconds staring after it in disbelief, his jaw hanging loose, before regaining his composure. A flurry of fumbling activity followed as he wrestled the rifle off his back. The Lee-Enfield was loaded, and the sound of the bolt being worked back and then forward, chambering a round, was a series of clicks which seemed like the ticking of a clock, counting down to an impending death.

Tom's father lifted the rifle to his shoulder. Tom felt his whole body tense in anticipation, watching that fleeing figure reach the far edge of the serac's overhang, about to disappear around a vast bank of snow. His father had only a moment to take the shot. The range was several hundred yards. Tom had seen him make such shots before on moving targets, and those smaller than the yeti, which was ten feet tall and four times the bulk of a man.

His father tracked the beast with the Lee-Enfield's iron sights, the rifle panning left to right in a fluid motion. He was in his element, the experienced hunter and expert marksman. Tom thought he cut a dashing figure, a hero in an adventure tale, rather than an abusive and emotionally distant father. All the years of conflict between them seemed to melt from his mind like snow in the sun, trickling into a stream which washed his heart clean. Suddenly it was easy to hope for something nobler for them, a fate which wasn't dark, but bright.

He saw the glamour of the hunt, the masculinity of the hunter. How he longed to hold the rifle himself, take that shot, desperate to become a man.

My time will come, he thought with certainty as he turned to look at the yeti. The window of opportunity was closing. With joyous anticipation he eagerly awaited the bang which would fell the creature.

But the shot never came.

"What do you think you're doing, you mad old goat?" said Tenzing, knocking the rifle aside.

"What I came here to do," said Tom's father, lifting the rifle again.

Tenzing grabbed the stock in one hand, the barrel in the other. "You'll bring the serac down upon our heads if you fire that thing!" he said as he attempted to wrench the weapon free of the old man's grip.

Tom's father wasn't giving it up without a fight, his warrior's spirit roused and his hatred of Tenzing enflamed. With wiry muscles tensed, his neck bulging, he cursed the Sherpa vehemently, spittle flying as they struggled. Tenzing was the stronger man, however, and was about to win out when Tom's father kneed him in the balls. The Sherpa let go, doubling over with a sharp exhalation of air. He tried to gather himself, lunging at Tom's father, but the old man dashed aside, raised the rifle again to aim down the length of the serac.

The yeti was gone.

"You great oaf," he said. "I had him in my sights."

"Let it go, Father," said Tom. "You've seen it. That's enough. We've proven it's real."

"We've no proof without the beast's head!"

His father dashed forward in pursuit of the yeti, rifle held across his chest. Tom moved to go after him, but Tenzing held out an arm to stop him, the other cradling his hurt nuts.

"Stay back," said the Sherpa. With a dextrous motion he unhooked the rope connecting Tom to his father.

"But he'll be killed!" said Tom.

"That's what you want, isn't it?"

"No." The word was a single sob of fear born of exhaustion and emotional bankruptcy. Tom didn't know what he wanted anymore, but it certainly wasn't to see his father ripped apart by a yeti on the desolate slopes of Mount Everest. "Let me go. I need to save him."

"You cannot save him. He was lost the moment he caught the fever to kill."

"That thing will tear him limb from limb." Tom was near hysterical, fighting in Tenzing's strong arms, which were wrapped around him protectively.

"I told you. The yeti lets the mountain do the killing," said Tenzing, jutting his chin up at the ice shelf. Tom's father was marching beneath its overhang in single minded fury, scanning for the yeti, rifle held ready.

Tom heard a gentle sound, drifting on the breeze. For a moment he thought it was just the wind playing tricks on him, but there was a melody to it, something which spoke of intelligence. It was a warbling song of vibrating notes, building in intensity and rising in frequency.

Tenzing grunted in affirmation, grimly acknowledging that his suspicions had been correct but not pleased about it.

"What is that?" asked Tom as the noise got louder.

"It is the yeti," said Tenzing.

"It… it sounds like… almost like yodelling."

It was a haunting melody from the throat of a species thought to be long extinct or to have never existed. It was a call for aid from the mountain itself, a song of death and destruction.

Tom watched in mounting horror as the snow around them started to shift. Tenzing pulled him away, but he fought in his grasp.

"My father is out there," he said, knowing for sure he never wished his father dead, for all the animosity and trouble between them.

If he dies, I'll be an orphan.

But Tom was helpless to save his father. The old man had become aware of the danger he was in, glancing up at the trembling ice shelf of the serac, the terror writ plain upon his face. He made a run for it, but not towards Tom and Tenzing, not towards help and possible safety, but further away from them, in pursuit of the unseen yeti, yodelling the mountain down upon him.

He seeks to kill it before it kills him, thought Tom, shaking with indignation. He knew it was too late. The vast cacophony of the yeti's yodelling shook the serac loose, the ice shelf sliding down with a roar of its own.

Mind boiling with panic and mortal terror, Tom thought not of his father, or Tenzing, or anyone or anything but his own safety, scrambling back away from the rumbling avalanche. He rushed for the shelter of a large rock, his movements feeling far too slow, his brain moving fast on ahead, willing him to safety. Something picked him up from behind and threw him—whether it was Tenzing or a wave of snow and ice, Tom did not know. He fell hard into the lee of the rock. Something packed in hard against him.

There was a last moment where all was the bright whiteness of snow. Then everything went dark.

11

At first, there was a lot of noise, the avalanche continuing on down the mountain, gathering momentum with a deafening roar, the world around Tom shaking violently as if he was in a plane experiencing bad turbulence. Slowly the noise died away into a distant rumble, stopping and starting as isolated mini-avalanches gave way in the distance. Then, eventually, there was silence.

Silence and darkness—a void filled with nothing but the searing hot poker of fear Tom felt jabbing him in the base of his brain.

I'm buried alive.

There was a rock at his back, its rough, jagged surface digging into his skin through his clothes.

But at least I wasn't crushed to death by falling snow and ice. This rock protected me.

It was a long time before he gathered up the courage to move at all, afraid he'd trigger a snowfall which would fill the tiny hollow he inhabited. Eventually he couldn't stand the strain on his body, his muscles screaming at him to stretch. He shifted slightly, found he couldn't extend his legs but he could straighten his back if he kinked his neck to the side. He rolled his shoulders and stretched his arms, touching something which shifted at the contact.

Tom's whole body went tense, frozen in terror.

The yeti is in here with me.

He heard a snuffling sound, like a pig rooting through mud in search of slops.

Oh, God, it's going to eat me.

The mass next to him moved again. Tom couldn't see in the pitch blackness, but he could feel it expand, taking up more room in the close confines. He tried to shrink in response, coiling up to hide in his corner of the hollow.

"Master Tom, is that you?" asked a familiar voice.

It was Tenzing.

Tom breathed out a breath he hadn't known he'd been holding, his body unfurling in the same movement. He reached out with hands to touch Tenzing, afraid for a moment that this was some type of trick of the yeti, or, perhaps even worse, that it was a trick of his own mind, desperate for any companionship and help in this dark hole.

"Yes, it's me," said Tom. "Is that really you, Tenzing?"

He heard rather than saw Tenzing nod and he had to laugh at this. He imagined the Sherpa smiling in response.

"So, how do we get out of this?" asked Tom.

"We're through the worst of it, waiting for the avalanches to stop. Now it's time to dig ourselves out. Pray to your god that the snow isn't too thick above our heads."

"Lucky for this rock."

"Yes, lucky for us. I fear for the others, including your father—he was right beneath the serac."

Tom trembled in the darkness. "You think he's dead."

"The serac is unforgiving when it falls, sweeping any in its path from the mountain like fleas from its back."

"The yeti set a trap, lured him on."

"Yes, it is cunning. We knew this."

"And yet you let my father go on, always on, knowing he was going to die."

"You knew it too."

"But I couldn't stop him. You could of though. You could have said no more and gone home. He would have had to go back."

Tenzing shifted in the dark. "Do not push me, Master Tom. I have been pushed too far already, lost control once. For that I am ashamed. But we are all at the mercy of our fate. I had to continue."

"Now what? How do we continue from here?"

"We don't. The bile has been purged. Your father's restless soul is at peace. We can go home at last."

"He was the only family I had left," said Tom, feeling utterly desolate, alone. Tenzing put a hand on his shoulder. It felt heavy, like a burden rather than a comfort.

"We'll look for him, but do not hope."

"And the other Sherpas?"

"They know to dig themselves out. They do so, as we do so, or they are already dead and buried in the snow."

"How do we dig ourselves out of here? I've lost my pick."

"There is a folding shovel in my backpack," said Tenzing, twisting to present his back to Tom, who rummaged around blindly in the pack until he got it.

"And now?"

"We take turns digging and hope the sun still shines when we break through."

"*If* we break through," corrected Tom.

He heard Tenzing nod in the darkness, but sensed no smile.

***

It wasn't easy, nor was it quick, the shovel awkward to wield in the confined space. Tom took tiny scoops, trying to find somewhere to store the snow.

"Put it behind you," advised Tenzing, indicating with the beam of his flashlight, "and then the second man pushes it back behind them with their hands. We burrow through like the marmot."

And they did, switching places when the digger got exhausted. Sometimes they were both too tired to carry on and they had a short nap. When Tom woke up he panicked in the claustrophobic darkness, screaming and kicking. Waking with a start, Tenzing cursed him out at first, and then soothed him by placing the oxygen mask on his face.

"Take a few deep breaths, Master Tom."

"If it wasn't for our oxygen tanks we'd be long dead," Tom said, handing the mask to Tenzing for his turn. Then they squeezed off the valve, hoarding the precious gas.

"Yes. Best we don't speak from now on to conserve air, and that goes for the screaming too."

"Hey, at least I've stopped wetting the bed."

"A small mercy," Tenzing deadpanned, went back to digging.

Finally, the snow ahead was no longer a blank wall of blackness—it had a tint of bluish yellow light to it. This grew in brightness as they forged on ahead, greatly encouraged, until the snow and ice was as thin as a pane of glass, the sun shining beyond. Tenzing punched through with his gloved hand and fresh, frigid air rushed in.

"It's still daylight," said Tom in wonder, crowding up next to Tenzing to peer through the hole.

"It's the next day," said Tenzing, widening the hole by scraping its edges with the shovel's blade.

"God, it's easy to lose track of time in a situation like that. Here, move aside, I think I can squeeze out that hole now."

"Patience, I need to get out too."

"Let me go and I can help dig from the outside."

"True," said Tenzing, shuffling to the side.

It was a tight squeeze, but Tom was desperate to be out of that hole. He wriggled and fought his way out, grinding the snow loose with his twisting body. With a final heave, he got free and fell in the snow.

The relief was immediate and overwhelming, the space around him feeling infinite. The Himalayas stretched on forever. The sun shone on his face. His heart fluttered in his chest, longing to fly away. His mind was blank except one ecstatic thought.

I'm alive.

He started to sob, releasing all his fear and tension.

"Hey, I thought you said you'd dig me out," said Tenzing. Tom wiped the tears from his face with his gloves, looked back at the hole. Seeing how pitifully small it was, and the space beyond, he quaked to think of what might have been.

That could have been my tomb.

"Sorry," he said, breaking into a smile because Tenzing was grinning like an idiot. He took up the shovel and started to dig.

12

Getting out of the hole was only half the battle. As soon as they were both free they scouted around and found their situation was desperate. The landscape had been wiped clean by the snow, a blank slate of whiteness with no recognisable features, all of it buried deep by the avalanche. They were utterly alone, far from any help, with only themselves to rely on.

"The others are dead," said Tenzing with grim certainty. "They would have got themselves out if it were possible."

"They could be in a pocket, surviving on their oxygen tanks," said Tom, gripping the shovel, willing to try.

Tenzing shook his head. "They would have done as we have done, fought to get themselves out. These were skilled and determined men."

"Maybe if we call out, they'll hear us. They could be close to the surface."

Tenzing grabbed Tom, as if to forestall him doing anything rash. "You'll bring the rest of the mountain down upon us," he whispered, as if even talking normally would trigger another avalanche.

"Maybe they already got out, abandoned us as we're abandoning them," sneered Tom, shucking off Tenzing's grasp and plodding around in the snow in search of signs.

"I wouldn't blame them if they did."

Tom ignored him, kept searching further along where the serac had once been, now a huge drift of fallen snow and ice. It continued for some way down the mountain, having gathered momentum, torn huge chunks of the frozen ice cliffs and banks of snow away, sent them tumbling hundreds of yards or more, disappearing with distance into a haze of fog below.

"There are a lot of clouds," said Tom. "I can't see the valley floor."

"We are cut off in a world above the world. This is the realm of the yeti," said Tenzing, joining him.

Tom trembled, and not only from the biting cold, the wind cutting through his clothes. "You think it's still about, hunting us?"

"I do not know. Does the hunter ever stop hunting?"

"What do you mean?"

Tenzing pointed along the fallen serac. There was a hole in the snow there.

"Father!" shouted Tom, ignoring Tenzing's advice to keep quiet. The mountain rumbled in complaint, the sound of his voice echoing back at them, but there was no further avalanche.

"No, Master Tom, wait," said Tenzing, wading through the deep snow, his bigger size impeding him.

Tom, buoyed by the possibility his father had survived and dug himself out of the snow, seemed to float above the ground, his feet barely touching it as he sprinted towards the hole. As he approached it, he slowed, alerted by an unconscious instinct. The hole was too big, much bigger than the narrow burrow he and Tenzing had escaped through. And a stench rose up from it, one unfamiliar to Tom but which touched a primordial part of his brain.

It was death.

Part bitter blood, part rotting gore, all nauseating horror—the smell rose up like a physical presence, warding him off. He recoiled from it. Falling into Tenzing's arms as he came up behind, Tom looked up at the Sherpa's face and saw the terror written in his lined features. Tom's blood froze.

If Tenzing's afraid, then surely we're in great danger, if not already dead, a pair of walking carcasses about to be butchered for meat.

To add to the horror of the smell was another sensation, tickling Tom's ears in a way which made him forget his fear for a moment, his curiosity piqued. The sound of breaking twigs made him loosen his grip on Tenzing's jacket, step forward toward the hole.

Father's in there, making himself a fire. That smell is the meat he's going to cook.

Tom heard slurping.

He's boiled a kettle and is drinking his tea.

These thoughts combined into one final, relieving conclusion.

Father is alive!

Tom darted forward.

"No," said Tenzing, but his voice was faraway to Tom, whose attention was entirely fixated on the hole. The sounds from it stopped abruptly as he reached the edge, looked down into it. Tom's heart beat hard in his chest. He sucked in a hard breath, held it.

At the bottom of the hole lay his father. The old man was torn into gory chunks, his blood splattered across the walls of the icy hole, trickling down to pool in the bottom. His decapitated head floated on the surface of this shallow puddle of red liquid, staring up at Tom in mute accusation, eyes wide and glassy, mouth open in a silent scream.

Warm piss jetted down Tom's leg as he released his breath. The hot ammonia stink of it drew the attention of the hole's other occupant. It was a primal terror from an ancient age—the yeti.

It ceased snapping bones and slurping marrow, lifted its head from its meal to gaze up at Tom. There was a pregnant pause where he could see the creature in great detail, especially the face, which seemed almost human, and certainly ape-like, with a high forehead and heavy brows. The eyes were keen and intelligent, yet piercing and feral, seeing in Tom not a fellow traveller of the Earth but merely fresh meat.

There was evidence enough of its hunger for flesh in the thing's protruding mouth, smeared with the grisly remains of Tom's father. The blood stained its skin darker. Gore matted its white fur. In its massive gorilla hands were broken shards of human bone.

Those huge hands... My father didn't dig his way out, the yeti dug its way in.

The monster's jaws opened wide in a feral snarl to reveal huge, sharp incisor teeth. Tom could smell the carnal stench of its breath, wafting up to meet him. His mind screamed at him to turn and run, but his body was frozen in place.

The yeti was the first to move.

With a series of powerful leaps it bounded upwards, bouncing from wall to wall with great strength and agility. Tom turned to run but he was too slow. The yeti sprang after him like a charging gorilla, grabbed him by a leg. Tom felt something in his leg give way with a fragile snap in the crushing grip of the meaty hand. He screamed, not in pain but in horrified shock, aware he was about to die.

The yeti swung him around by his broken leg, hurled him down into the hole. He landed with the sound of more bones breaking, but they weren't his own, they were his father's, the ribcage of the dead man collapsing to cushion his fall. Tom kept screaming, thrashing about in the shredded remains of his father's corpse, quickly covered head to toe in the slush of blood and melted snow. His arm struck something hard, but he didn't register what it was, his mind filled with nothing but blind panic and mortal terror. He felt like he was being electrocuted, such was the way his brain and body convulsed in horror at his disgusting situation and impending violent death.

Any ability to try to calm down at all, think of a way out of his situation, was cut off as the yeti appeared at the lip of the hole several metres above his head. From this perspective it was even more of a towering monster than when seen from above. Tom kept kicking and punching at the air in a vain attempt to free himself from the gory mess of his father's body. His knuckles rapped that hard object again. This time he reflexively reached out to grab whatever it was. It was a heavy stick of some type.

He pulled it close, aware it wouldn't be any use in warding off the yeti, but relieved to at least have the illusion of being able to put up a fight. This allowed him to calm down just a touch, enough to bring him back from the edge of insanity. This growing clarity nearly yielded once more to fear as the yeti bent down, eyes fixed on Tom's, and started climbing down the hole, licking its lips, clearly relishing the thought of the meal to come.

Damn it, where's Tenzing?

"Probably already dead," he said. Sadness washed over him to think these were his last words. He looked at his father's decapitated head, thought of something more fitting. "You've killed us both, you dumb bastard."

The yeti loomed over him, arms and legs splayed to grip the walls of the hole. Its silhouette blotted out the sun's light like a spider closing in on the prey caught in its web. Tom clutched the stick tighter across his chest, only then realising what it was—the Lee-Enfield rifle.

He didn't think. Acting out of instinct he repeated well practiced movements. The bolt was slippery with blood, but it slid smoothly. Angling the barrel up at the yeti, the monster frowned in curiosity.

Tom shot it in the face.

The yeti reared up, gripping the icy lip of the hole, bellowing its mighty lungs out, the sound impossibly loud in the confined space. The noise struck Tom like a physical blow, stunning him for a moment, so he was slow to work the bolt again. But he fought through the aural onslaught, got another round chambered. The yeti looked at him, having heard this tell-tale click clack of the weapon before, a prelude to the searing pain it clearly felt now.

It glared down at Tom, half of its face missing. He could see its pink tongue lolling around through the hole in its jaw, shattered teeth swimming in blood which dripped like drool out of the cavernous wound. The left eye socket was shattered, a pulped crater filled with gory jelly.

But the right eye was filled with hate, as well as an emotion he did not expect from the beast—fear.

Tom felt a wave of empathy wash over him. He squeezed the trigger anyway. There was a click, but no bang—the weapon was jammed with his father's gore. He almost panicked but knew this would provoke the monster. Sensing weakness, it would leap down and crush him with its weight. Instead, Tom shook the rifle at it like a shaman using his voodoo stick to banish a demon. The yeti backed off slowly at first, and Tom worried it might see through his ploy, become aware he couldn't repeat the grievous wound he had already dealt it.

How smart is this thing really?

Realising this meal wasn't worth it, the yeti swung around, gripped the lip of the hole with its two massive hands, and hauled itself out, disappearing from view.

Obviously not intelligent enough to work out the rifle had jammed, but aware it had the power to kill it, Tom thought with relief. Still, he couldn't rest yet. With the last of his strength and adrenaline he fought with the bolt until the jam was cleared, using his finger to hook out the gore in the chamber. He wasn't sure it would fire, but he chambered a round anyway, pointed the rifle at the circle of sky at the top of the hole. Time passed. The pain in his leg started to build and his arms shook with weakness.

Just when he was about to lower the rifle, collapse into the revolting filth, a silhouette appeared at the entrance of the hole, blotting out the light. His reflexes were slow, but he pulled the trigger a second later, aimed directly at the dark shadow.

The rifle jammed again, no shot fired. Tom dropped the weapon in disgust, fed up with life and ready to die.

"Are you still alive, Master Tom?"

It was Tenzing, not the yeti, who was climbing into the hole. To Tom's own surprise he felt no surge of relief, no happiness, just a deepening numbness. He made a strangled, croaking sound like a frog.

"Don't worry, the yeti has fled," said Tenzing. "Are you hurt?"

"My leg," said Tom. He tried to lift an arm to indicate which one but it was no use. He had nothing left.

Tenzing inspected both, carefully probing each in turn with his fingers through the bloody slush filling the bottom of the hole. "Tsk, tsk, we're in trouble. A broken leg this far up the mountain is very serious."

"We're lucky," managed Tom, "that the yeti didn't kill us."

"You call this luck? I told you, the yeti lets the mountain do the killing. If we get back to base camp it will be a miracle."

Tom swallowed hard, his throat rough with razor blades. Tenzing reached up the side of the hole where the snow wasn't smattered with blood, scraped some off, put it in Tom's mouth.

"You're a real ray of sunshine, Tenzing," he said, smiling wanly.

Tenzing didn't share his smile, his brow furrowed in concern. "I'm a realist. Our chances are not good."

"Speaking of realistic chances, how did you survive the yeti's attack?"

Tenzing snorted. "Not all of us are so stupid as to rush up to a yeti when it is eating."

"You tried to stop me."

"Yes, I did. And when you wouldn't listen, I did what any sane person would do. I went to hide."

"Where?"

"In our hole. Where else? I covered the entrance with snow and prayed the yeti didn't smell me."

"Surely it would have followed your tracks."

"Ah, probably it did," said Tenzing with a shrug. "Maybe it thought they belonged to you. They're intelligent but I've heard their eyesight isn't great."

"More likely it knew you were in there, kept on ice, a meal it could save for later while it came back and finished me." Tom shivered at the thought, grimaced at the grisly remains filling the hole.

"If that is the case, then you have saved my life, my friend. If you didn't drive it off with the rifle it would have returned, dug me up like your father."

Tom sagged, weighed down by grief. He did his best not to look at the decapitated head bobbing in the melted red snow. "You think he was alive when the yeti found him?"

"No, I don't. He was right under the serac. He would have been crushed instantly when it fell. That's how the yeti hunts. You heard it call to bring down the avalanche. Then it sniffs out the corpse, digs down into the snow to find its meal."

"Why, when it is so much stronger than a man? I've never been so terrified of something in my life."

"Because it knows men use tools, men have weapons. It has learned that lesson yet again today. I saw it flee. You wounded it grievously—a trail of blood leads up over the mountain."

"It'll probably come back for the others eventually. Dig them up and eat them."

Tenzing's face twisted in angry disgust and Tom wished he'd not said anything.

"Yes," said Tenzing. "And that could so easily have been our fate as well." Somehow he managed to pull a smile out from somewhere deep inside. "But as you say, we are lucky, we are alive, and that is something."

"So you're an optimist now?" asked Tom, heartened despite the pain in his leg.

"I let myself be dragged along in your father's wake, lured by his promises of money. Now he is dead and I am free, as are you, Master Tom."

Tom laughed. "If I live through this I will be a rich man."

"Yes, a rich *man*. No one will call you boy ever again."

"You'll not abandon me, will you, Tenzing?"

"You saved my life, shooting the yeti. I'll get you down off this mountain, if I am able. I owe you that much."

"And I'll owe you a big tip."

They both laughed.

"You think it's possible we can climb down with my leg?" Tom asked, wincing from the pain as he tried to sit up.

Tenzing stood. "I'll get some rope from my pack. We'll splint your leg with the shovel. I'll be right back. Don't go anywhere."

"I'll try not to."

Tenzing climbed out of the hole. Standing on its lip he looked back down at Tom and said, "Brace yourself. This is going to be an ordeal."

13

Everest Base Camp, 2011

"And it was, believe me, it was," said Tom, finishing his story. He took a drink from his servant. "Thanks, Buddy. Cheers to you all." He lifted his glass to those sitting around the table.

The gathered bunch of mountain climbers and miscellaneous camp workers raised their own drinks in salute as the wind outside whipped the tent walls about. "Cheers," they said and drank.

Tom was aware they were saluting a story well told, rather than actually believing a word he had said. To them, the yeti was nothing but a myth. These modern sceptics thought themselves too smart to fall for such tall tales. He didn't care. Years of hunting cryptids had taught him one thing—it was damn hard to convince anyone of anything. So he didn't worry about other people's opinions. Not living ones anyway. And he had his own means of making sure history at least was on his side. In time, no one would doubt that he was the greatest hunter of creatures most thought it impossible to prove even existed, let alone kill.

"So you didn't even kill the yeti?" asked one woman, her brow furrowed. Tom noticed she hadn't drunk the toast, didn't have a drink in front of her.

There's always one in every crowd who has to grill me, he thought.

"No, the yeti won that round. But at least I got away, lived to fight another day," he said, knocking back the remainder of his drink and handing the glass off to his man.

"So that's why you're back in the Himalayas, to find the yeti that killed your father decades ago?"

"If you think I'm motivated by revenge, I'm more annoyed it broke my leg. I still have a bit of a limp."

There were polite chuckles from the others.

"I think you're motivated by madness," said the woman.

Tom smiled indulgently. She didn't return the smile, just raised her eyebrows in challenge.

At least she's very pretty, thought Tom.

He leant forward, rested his bottom lip on his knuckles. She held his gaze.

And she's got spirit.

This gave him an idea.

"What's your name, love?" he asked.

"Layla, and don't call me love."

"Alright, Layla. If you're so sure the yeti doesn't exist, why don't you come with me up the mountain, see for yourself?"

Everyone at the table turned their eyes on her, watching how she would respond to the challenge.

"I came here to climb the highest peak in the world, not go off on some wild goose chase," she said.

"Don't worry," Tom countered calmly. "You can climb the mountain at the same time. It's what I intend to do."

Layla scoffed. “Yeah, right. You’re the richest man here, by some margin from what I hear—as if you have any real interest in mountaineering.”

“I’ve climbed it before.”

“That story you just told us? It was pure nonsense. You’ve got no proof any of that happened.”

“Well, my father is definitely dead. It’s hard to survive with your head ripped off.”

This got a few louder laughs, as well as some facial expressions to show that perhaps that was poor taste. No one said as much though.

Most people keep their opinions to themselves, awed by my wealth. They like to keep their options open, maybe have a chance of getting some of it.

“I’m surprised you didn’t take it home and mount it on your wall,” said Layla.

But not this one, thought Tom, intrigued.

“No,” he said, “we just pushed some snow into the hole, buried him up on the mountain. He’s still up there, as far as I know. Unless the yeti came back for seconds.”

He looked around the table to bask in the smiles he got in return for his wit. They helped him hide from the dark trauma of that memory. Something he still carried to this day.

I hope to finally banish him this time. I’m sick of carrying his ghost around.

“It was quite a story, I’ll give you that,” said Layla, not letting up. “But it hardly makes you qualified to be leading a team up one of the most challenging peaks in the world.”

"I've been on the mountain other times as well," he said.

She crossed her arms and rolled her eyes. "Didn't find the yeti those times either? What a surprise."

Well, that little act just makes her more attractive, thought Tom.

"They were just research, training, information gathering. My father went in half-cocked. I like to be more thorough," he said.

There was a laugh from someone in the tent, just a single guffaw. Tom twisted in his seat. It came from his servant, Buddy. Tom gave the big man a frown—he returned a smile like an indulgent uncle and went back to pretending to be busy with the food and drinks.

"Now you think you're ready for the push to the summit?" asked Layla.

Tom turned back to face her, meeting her gaze levelly. "The only summit which really matters."

This brought some cries of indignation from the mountaineers present, both those who had climbed the highest peak before, and those who were here to fulfil a lifelong dream. Tom waved them off like pesky flies.

"As you've pointed out," he said to Layla. "I'm no mountaineer. Climbing the mountain is just incidental, a means to the end."

"You're a yeti hunter then?"

"I consider myself more of a cryptid collector."

14

"All preposterous nonsense, of course," said Layla to a friend as they left the communal dining tent. She cast a sidelong glance at Tom. He smiled at her, gave her a nod. She shook her head slightly, kept walking over the rocky ground.

Tom put his hands on his hips, took in the scene, breathing in the fresh air. A multitude of colourful tents shook in the breeze, people moving among them on their various tasks, most related in one way or another to the business of climbing or supporting the climbers. All around the mountains hemmed them in. The imagined weight of these made his shoulders hunch, as if carrying their millions of tonnes on his back. He found himself feeling claustrophobic despite the vast open space. It wasn't easy to be back here, memories of being buried under ice and snow flooding back.

"Not going to be an easy one to tame," said Buddy, coming up beside Tom and jutting his chin after Layla. He was polishing a beer glass with a rag, which he tossed nonchalantly across his shoulder, flashed his boss a smile.

"What's that? Her?" said Tom, taking the glass out of Buddy's hand and holding it up to the light to inspect it. "I'm here for the yeti, not her."

Buddy gave him a dubious 'I've heard that one before' look.

Tom shrugged. "Well, if there's time for both."

"There isn't. We've got a lot of preparations to make," said Buddy.

"I'll leave that in your capable hands, and in those of the Sherpas."

Buddy growled like a loyal dog.

"Don't get your knickers twisted, Buddy," said Tom. "Like all very rich men, I have a penchant for hiring expert help. Why do you think I pay you so much, eh?"

"To do all the work?"

"It's my job to spot talent and employ it."

"And to pull the trigger and take the credit."

Tom grimaced, handed the glass back to Buddy. "You missed a spot."

***

"Oh, funny running into you here," Tom said to Layla, as if he hadn't carefully orchestrated it, using Buddy as a lookout and a series of elaborate bird calls to communicate between them.

"I eat here every day," she said, looking like she saw through his false casualness.

Yes, I had Buddy find that out too, thought Tom.

Layla went to get in the line outside the tent which served as a restaurant, a semi-permanent structure that catered to the climbers with a variety of hot meals.

"There's no need for that," said Tom, craning his neck to look over the heads of those in line. He caught the eye of the restaurateur, a Nepalese man, with a click of his fingers, getting an enthusiastic nod in return. "What would you like to eat? It's on me."

She raised her eyebrows. "And in exchange?"

He laughed it off, hurt by her bluntness. It was ruining his suave act. "No exchange, but if you'd do me the honour of sitting with me in the dining tent, I would very much enjoy your company."

"How very noble of you," she deadpanned. "Okay. A red curry with rice, very hot, with lots of vegetables, no meat."

"You're vegetarian?"

"And I suppose you are too?"

"I do happen to be, yes."

"That's unusual, right, for a hunter?"

"I don't eat yetis."

"No, they just eat your father." She gave a single bark of laughter, which Tom thought unnecessarily cruel. He almost turned and walked away, instead he made a face, which she obviously chose to ignore, or maybe to capitalise upon, for she turned the screw even tighter, doubling down. "That's convenient, isn't it? The yeti disposing of your father, I mean. I'm sure you didn't benefit financially from that little misadventure."

Tom started to shake with rage, his face going red.

"It puts a whole new twist on the phrase 'eat the rich,' doesn't it?" she said with relish.

Tom's anger turned to horror, images flashing before his eyes. He saw the yeti ripping his father into pieces, gulping him down. The glassy eyes of the decapitated head stared at him in disapproval.

He blinked heavily to clear the vision. It was replaced by Layla's smug face. He took a faltering step away from her. She cocked an eyebrow, waiting for his witty comeback. He had none.

"You can buy your own damn meal," he growled, stalking off.

15

Tom sat alone in the dining tent, sipping discontentedly at the drink Buddy had made then left, dismissed with a gesture and a grunt. He shook the ice in the glass with a tinkle, the only sound besides the ghostly moan of the wind through the mountains. The interior of the big tent felt lonelier and emptier than even the wide open spaces outside, which at night time could feel barren, no matter how many lights the generators powered. He had only a single candle upon the table—mood lighting—and this made his world feel even smaller, closing in on him until he felt like he was back up the mountain, buried in that hole. It didn't help that the table before him was small, confining him further. It was set with a red tablecloth and a red rose in a glass vase. Tom stared at these in the candlelight, the vibrant colour shimmering and dancing, seeming to flow.

Oh, God, the blood.

He threw back his drink in a single gulp, the ice clicking against his teeth, bringing back memories of the bitter cold awaiting him up the mountain. The liquor warmed his stomach, though it was of no comfort, somehow reminding him of the yeti gulping down the gory remains of his father.

Tom let out a feral snarl as if to frighten the beast away, adding to the banishment by slamming the empty glass down on the table. It rattled the fine porcelain plates and shining silverware—a dinner set for two. The noise jangled Tom from his reverie, made him notice the tent flap had opened. The howl of the wind outside got louder, the sound of it making him shiver more than the gust of cold air.

That cursed yodelling which brought down the mountain.

He heard clicking footsteps in the gloom, boots on the plastic floorboards, and looked up at his uninvited guest, a silhouette at the far end of the tent.

"I paid good money to have the dining tent to myself tonight. I will thank you to leave," he said.

"No one paid me anything," said Layla, stepping forward into the meagre illuminated circle of the candle's flickering flame.

Tom shot to his feet, pushing his chair back. "Oh, it's you."

"Don't stand on my account. Am I intruding on some private moment?" she asked, indicating the table and general surrounds with one hand. With the other she clutched a pair of sealed plastic takeaway containers, with disposal wooden cutlery on top held there with a thumb.

"Private, yes," said Tom, blushing. "But you could never intrude." He went around the table, pulled the second chair out for her.

She gave him a wry look, a hint of a smile tugging at one corner of her lips, and sat down as he pushed the chair in for her. He went and sat opposite her.

"So this is all for my benefit?" she asked, laughter bubbling on her speech.

He flushed an even deeper shade of crimson, matching the tablecloth. She leaned forward, pushed the rose and vase aside to make space.

"It's entirely unnecessary," she continued, cracking the plastic lids of her meal.

His heart skipped a beat, suddenly hopeful. "Oh?"

"Yes, because it's entirely ludicrous."

He felt his heart fall into his guts with a splash.

She tipped the contents of her meal containers onto the porcelain plate and looked around for somewhere to put them. Finding nowhere, she shrugged and put the empties on the floor.

"These are utterly useless, right?" she said, similarly discarding the wooden cutlery and taking up a silver fork. It flashed as it caught the candlelight, mirrored in her brilliant, white smile. It gave her a mischievous air Tom found intriguing. He leaned forward, pretending to be interested in her meal.

"That looks good," he said.

"Yeah, it is." She was already digging in, speaking around mouthfuls.

It was Tom's turn to raise his eyebrows, but he shrugged off her bad manners, held his hand up and clicked his fingers. Buddy materialised out of thin air, standing next to the table. He had steaming hot food on a silver tray, which he served up onto Tom's plate.

"Christ, where did he come from?" said Layla. "Hey, are those papadams?"

"Thanks, Buddy. And yes, would you like one?" said Tom, indicating for Buddy to offer her the tray. He did so.

"He calls you Buddy?" she asked the large, ungainly servant.

"That's his name," said Tom.

"He can talk for himself," she snapped at him.

"That's my name," said Buddy.

Layla scooped up some of her curry with a papadam, shovelled it whole into her mouth. "Weird name. Wow, this curry is hot."

Buddy's face was blank, totally unreactive.

"Comes from the Gaelic word *bhodaich*," said Tom.

"And that means?" she asked.

"Old man," said Buddy.

"You don't look that old."

"He's older than me. I suppose that's all that matters," said Tom. "It also means ghost, which I personally find much more fitting."

"And Gaelic? You're Scottish, Buddy?" asked Layla. "You have some type of accent."

"Australian, actually," he said.

"But he's a man of the world, like me, aren't you, Buddy?" said Tom.

"Yes, sir."

Layla laughed, warming to what she seemed to take as playacting. "He calls you sir and everything?"

Buddy said nothing.

"When appropriate," said Tom.

Buddy glanced at him. Tom nodded with a slow blink of assent. Buddy gave a curt little bow of his head, melted back into the shadows.

"So, Buddy's your… what?" asked Layla, tucking back into her food.

"Butler," said Tom, taking up his knife and fork, carefully cutting up a portion of food and only eating when he had ceased speaking.

"He certainly acts the part." She looked around, unable to find the man anywhere in the tent. "With you calling him Buddy, you'd assume he's more of a friend, a companion."

Tom chuckled, putting down his cutlery. "He's that too. He shares all my adventures."

"Right…" she said dubiously. She shook her fork at him like a wagging finger. "The cryptid hunting, yeah?"

"Cryptid collecting."

"But you do kill them, don't you?"

"I do."

"To what end?"

"I don't know if that's something I'm willing to divulge on a first date."

"Fresh of you to assume there'll be a second."

Not if you keep shovelling that bloody food into your mouth like that, thought Tom. He grinned feebly.

"Why don't you tell me a little about yourself?" he asked.

"Me?" She paused from eating for a moment, picked a napkin, burped into it.

How very charmingly polite, he thought.

"I'm a journalist," she said and went back to eating.

"Oh…" said Tom, his tone inflecting downwards.

"Oh? What oh? You don't like journalists?"

Tom caught himself, tried to wave it off as if it were nothing. "Journalists and I, well, we haven't exactly seen eye to eye in the past."

"Because of the lying, right? About the yeti and all the other monsters you claim to have hunted down. Yes, journalists prefer to deal in the truth."

Tom was so taken aback by her forthrightness—not to mention how ridiculous he found the concept of a journalist being interested in the truth—that he guffawed.

"I took the liberty of looking you up after your little story time earlier," she said. "Not easy, is it? Being called out for what you are."

"I might be a lot of things, my dear, but a liar I am not."

"Got no proof, though, have you?"

He frowned deeply in consternation. "I was going to save this for our second date."

"Look, this isn't a date."

"What is it then? An interview?"

"Fuck no. I'm just trying to eat my meal somewhere out of the wind, unlike those poor bastards you supposedly paid to stay out of here. Did you think you could woo me by buying out the entire restaurant?"

"It had crossed my mind," he admitted.

"Well, uncross it. All of it seems like a grand gesture until you think of how it inconveniences others. What about the bunch of sad looking people squatting on a rock in the wind right now, trying to scoff down their meals? Bet you didn't think of them, did you?"

"I'm not an idiot. I take calculated gambles."

"I get it, because you've some romantic notion of yourself as some type of globetrotting adventurer? Give me a break. You think I've not met guys like you before?"

"You've never met anyone like me before."

"Everyone is an archetype. Either that or they're a blend of different archetypes. Unique as a combination, sure, but their constituent parts are well mapped out and predictable. There's nothing new under the sun. I learned that much in my years as a journalist."

"So you're here chasing some story?"

"No, this is my holiday. I'm here to challenge myself. I want to see if I can best the world's tallest mountain."

"This conversation is off the record then?"

"It might surprise you, Sir Tom, but the world isn't automatically interested in every little thing you say and do just because you're rich."

"The world might not be interested now, but they will be one day."

"And why's that?"

He smiled a wolf's grin. "Because I have proof."

16

"I'll need to get Buddy to bring in some equipment," said Tom. "Would you like a glass of wine while we wait?" He raised his hand to click his fingers.

"No thanks, and I wish you wouldn't do the whole summoning the help routine. It's pretty boring rich guy stuff, don't you think?"

He lowered his hand, abashed. Buddy appeared anyway carrying an electronic device in a black case. He put it down, begun clearing the dinner things from the table to make room for it.

"Well, he's obviously been listening," she said, chagrined. "This is hardly the private date you professed this to be."

"I thought you said this wasn't a date?"

"I don't think anyone in the world would count me buying my own dinner followed by you ambushing me in the mess tent a date."

"I didn't ambush you."

"Did you ask permission?"

"No. You're free to go at any time."

"Of course I'm free to go, you pompous oaf," she snapped. She crossed her arms with a huff. "What is all this anyway?"

Buddy didn't answer, he just set the box on the table, started to unfold it.

"It's a holographic projector," said Tom.

"And that's proof of what exactly? That you can afford fancy gadgets? What are you going to do, summon up holograms of various cryptids you've hunted?"

Buddy gave Tom a questioning look.

Tom furrowed his brows in response, said, "Yes, yes, Buddy, we'll skip that part of the presentation, go straight to the meat of it."

Layla let out a single mocking bark of mirth. "I was right? Geez, is this how you try to impress all the girls?"

"I'll have you know this is a very special occasion," said Tom, getting very annoyed. "I don't show this to just anyone. In fact, I had no intention of showing anyone any of this in my own lifetime."

"It is a special occasion, miss," said Buddy.

"I'm sure you've both got this routine down pat," she replied. "I'm one of a kind woman, a unique beauty, blah, blah, blah." She waved her hands to hurry it along. "So let's have it then. What's the big hubbub?"

"I never called you a unique beauty," said Tom, getting up and giving Buddy a nod.

"Try not to double down on being a total dick, won't you?" she said.

Tom ignored her, flaring his arm out like a showman unveiling their latest spectacle as the holographic projector was activated. "*This* is a unique beauty!"

The shadows retreated like an opening curtain, replaced by blue light which sparkled in the air, danced across the wall. At first it looked like a laser show, the beams catching particles of dust as they floated in the air. Then it seemed as if Tom was showing her some type of star map, the constellations slowly rotating around the room in three dimensions.

"What is this?" asked Layla, standing so she was submerged in the holographic lights. They traced blue patterns across her face where she broke the beams.

"It's a genetic map. Several in fact," said Tom in hushed awe.

"You sound impressed with yourself, that's for sure. But what does that even mean?"

"It means, young woman," hissed Buddy, obviously reaching some threshold of patience as yet unseen by her, "that you are in the presence of the greatest hunter of all time."

Whether he meant himself or Tom wasn't exactly clear from his tone.

"I can hardly bow down to the greatness of something if it's not explained to me. I'm a journalist, not a genetic scientist," she said, hands raised as if surrendering.

"These," said Tom, pointing to a string of vertical lines in rows, "are strings of genetic code, complete maps of various cryptids I have hunted and killed."

Layla frowned, leaned in closer to the portion of the hologram closest to her. There were the fatter bands of light with blank spaces in between he'd indicated, but also long strings of tiny numbers and letters tied to them with thin lines. She whistled as if impressed. "If you say so."

"You asked for proof and here it is."

"Not exactly a body or anything like that a lay person can look at and touch."

"Trust me, even if I presented a body to the media, people would still be sceptical."

"Rightly so, if you're trying to convince everyone yetis are real. Why not capture a live one then?"

Tom laughed. "You've obviously never been face to face with an angry yeti before."

"Neither have you, you total fraud."

Buddy shook his head in disgust.

Layla saw this, softened a little, feeling some empathy for this long suffering servant at least. "I'm sure if you brought back a head people would have to listen."

"And mount it on my wall like some morbid trophy?" said Tom, his own disappointment growing. "Sounds like something my father would do. I'm not him."

"Going up Mount Everest to hunt a yeti sounds like something your father would do, did do, in fact. Yet here you are, repeating that mistake."

"You don't know what it's like. I regret showing you this now."

"What I don't know is what you hoped to achieve with this whole song and dance."

Buddy looked everywhere in the tent but at the two of them. Tom rubbed the back of his neck.

"I was hoping you might be impressed, I suppose," he said. "Foolish of me. I see that now."

"Without me being a professor of genetics I hardly see how that could have been the case. I'd just be taking your word for it. If you hadn't noticed, that hasn't been enough for me. Why not show this to a professional?"

"I don't want that, not in my lifetime."

"Oh, modesty now, is it? Or is it that you're a charlatan trying to get into my pants?"

"That's totally unfair, I—"

"If you had a living breathing yeti here in front of me I might be impressed. But what good is this?" She waved her hand through the hologram as if there was nothing there.

Tom took a series of long, deep breaths in and out, his eyes closed. When he opened them, he fixed her with a determined gaze, took a step towards her.

"These *are* living, breathing creatures, don't you see?" he said, clamping his hands together and giving them a shake as if to implore her to believe. "This here is the barghest from Northern England." He indicated a whole swathe of the genetic map with fingers splayed, his voice filled with wonder. "It is a monstrous black dog with huge claws and teeth. I shed more than a little of my own blood to get but a drop of its. And now here it is; the code which one day could bring that seemingly impossible creature back to life, make it possible. Even a sceptic like you couldn't deny it then, when they can clone a mating pair and breed them."

She shook her head in disbelief. "You want to clone it? That's a bit science fiction, isn't it?"

"Everything is possible given time. Technology is advancing. They cloned a sheep. Why not a barghest?"

"Because it's not real, Tom." She clapped her hands in front of his face with each word, as if trying to wake him up.

"This is a waste of time, sir," said Buddy, switching off the projector.

As the hologram disappeared, Tom seemed to deflate somewhat, his world contracting around him, the light restricted back to that single candle, flickering, almost guttering out, but providing a focal point which they all turned to. But then a gust through a gap in the tent blew even that out.

17

"Well, this is spooky," said Layla. The tent was in total darkness.

"Get a torch, will you, Buddy?"

"Already looking, sir."

"That weather is really something," said Layla. Outside, the wind howled like a banshee.

To Tom's ear though it took on a familiar sound, rising and falling in a set of notes he'd not heard in years, except in his dreams.

No, it cannot be.

He felt the cold fist of fear grab his spine in its grip, making his whole body go rigid.

"You hear that, sir?" asked Buddy.

"Oh, God," said Tom, the fear morphing into quaking terror. His voice broke like an adolescent as he asked, "You can hear it too?"

"It's just the wind," said Layla.

"Quiet!" hissed Tom.

They all stood in the darkness, everything silent except for a distant sound.

"Is that…" said Layla. "Is that yodelling?"

"Yes," said Tom, certain now. His blood ran cold. "It's the cry of the yeti."

***

A beam of white light cut the air like a flashing sword.

"Found it," said Buddy, shining the torch about.

Tom squinted into the light, his eyes playing tricks on him as his night vision was ruined, dark splotches and shapes moving about at the corners of his sight. In his mind each turned into the yeti, looming over him, waiting to drop down on him like an avalanche with all its weight. His knees knocked together in fear, and he had to fight hard to stop them, not totally successful. Layla noticed this.

"You don't really expect me to believe that sound is the yeti, do you?" she asked, incredulous. She looked at Buddy. Even his stoic façade was showing some signs of strain. This seemed to affect her somewhat, her eyes darting around the tent.

A huge roar tore through the air, the bellowing cry of an ancient monster.

Layla jumped into Tom's arms. He steadied at her touch, comforted by her warmth, but also finding resolve and courage in his subconscious desire to protect her.

"It's the mountain," he said, the words spoken intimately in her ear, quiet and insistent despite the loudness of the noise all around. "The yeti has called down the avalanche."

"But I thought you said it did that to hunt?" she asked, her mounting fear overriding her reason and scepticism.

"It never stops hunting," said Tom, reluctantly untangling her limbs from his own.

The roaring of the avalanche died away, the yodelling absent in its wake. Layla seemed to come to her senses, looked at him, embarrassed, straightening her clothing.

“I should be getting back to my tent,” she said. “I need my rest. My team is heading up the mountain tomorrow.”

“You’re not still going?” asked Tom.

“Are you?”

“Of course I am. But you heard the yeti. It’s out there, waiting.”

“There’s no need for this, Tom. It’s all just an act, right? Like a teenager going to see a scary movie with a girl in the hopes she’ll be frightened, curl up in your arms.”

“Damn it, Layla, this isn’t one of your archetypes.”

“No, it’s far more pathetic than that, because you’re a grown man. Goodnight, Tom. Goodnight, Buddy.”

“Ma’am,” said Buddy. Layla laughed at that, left the tent.

“Not your finest showing, sir,” Buddy said to Tom.

“Yes, I know. The holographic genetic map normally gets them.”

“At least we know the yeti is out there,” said Buddy with a rare smile. “Always nice to know we’re not wasting our time, have a chance to add to the collection.”

“Yes,” said Tom grimly, “if it doesn’t add you and me to its own first.”

18

Tom awoke to the sound of screaming. At first he thought it was a carryover from his dream, a familiar nightmare he often experienced, reliving his first encounter with the yeti.

Damn, but if I achieve nothing else but the banishment of that damn memory on this trip, I'll be satisfied.

But the sound wasn't a dream. The screaming was real, and it was coming from all around him.

By God, what's going on?

Buddy burst into his tent just as he fought his way out of his sleeping bag, shivering in the cold and reaching for clothes.

"Sir?" said Buddy, a dark silhouette against even greater darkness.

"Yes, I'm alright. Get a light on, will you?"

"Not a good idea, I'm afraid." Buddy somehow found the items of clothes Tom scrambled for in the dark, handed them to his employer one by one.

The screaming was accompanied by a terrible roaring, like a hungry, enraged lion set loose on the gladiators in the Colosseum.

"Another avalanche?" asked Tom.

"It's the yeti. It's here in the camp," said Buddy.

"What? That's impossible. Not this far down the mountainside. We're not even on the peak proper."

"I saw it."

"It would hardly be considered mythological if it ever attacked large groups of people at base camp, now would it?"

"I said *I saw it.*"

"Okay, okay, I believe you. You've hardly steered me wrong before." He grasped Buddy on the shoulder in a comradely gesture.

A terrible shrieking split the air, echoed by shouts of alarm. It was followed by a scream of awful pain, accompanied by a loud crunch.

"It's feeding?" asked Tom in horror, adrenaline pumping through his veins. Despite the fear, he found his mind growing clearer now the moment of crisis had come.

You live for this, you sick bastard, he thought of himself.

"On the mountaineers, yes," said Buddy. "Question is, do we let it have its fill, go after it in the morning, following the tracks, or do we face up to it now? My vote is on the former. If we keep silent, keep the light off, it'll probably pass us by."

Tom shook his head in the darkness.

No, if it has come down the mountain it's because it knows I'm here. It wants its revenge just as much as I do.

"Layla's out there," he said instead.

"Forget her," hissed Buddy. "She's not worth getting killed over. She doesn't even seem that interested in you."

"Because she thought I was lying. Now she'll know I wasn't. She'll have seen the yeti with her own eyes."

"You know that's no guarantee. Remember the aniwye? Those people saw *that* with their own eyes. They still had the audacity to say it was just a regular skunk later on, making you look like a fool."

"An aniwye does look a lot like a skunk, though, you have to admit."

"Yeah, but the size of a bear."

"We got it in the collection. There will be no doubt one day, after I'm dead."

"Let's not hurry that day along then, shall we? Live tonight, fight tomorrow. You don't have to go out there and play the hero."

"Give me the rifle," said Tom, holding his hands out. There was no question of which rifle he was referring to, or of Buddy not having brought it along with him, pre-empting his master's wishes, even when he thought they were ill-advised.

Buddy gave him the rifle. Tom's grip closed around the familiar shape of it, feeling instantly more at ease and sure of himself.

It was his father's Lee-Enfield .303.

"Let's go shoot a yeti in the face," he said.

"And save the girl," said Buddy with a sigh.

Tom shrugged as if it didn't matter. "If there's time."

***

Exiting the tent, a wall of noise and chaotic movement washed over Tom, spiking his adrenaline further. His heart beat so hard the corner of his eye twitched. Lights danced in the darkness, handheld torches and larger lamps shone this way and that as people ran in every direction, not knowing where the danger came from and which way led to safety.

Tom had the same problem. He heard the yeti roar, but the sound echoed off the mountains surrounding them, bounced back in a confusing barrage of terrifying noise. His sphincter tightened at the savage cry, the monster's call full of bestial fury. It was answered by screams—among them a woman's which sounded familiar.

"Layla!" shouted Tom and went to rush off. He was held back by a hand on his shoulder. It was Buddy. Tom looked at him and the man shook his head in the gloom. He was hunched over, an F88 Austeyr assault rifle held loose but alert in his hands as he scanned their surrounds.

"We don't know where the yeti is," said Buddy.

"But we can find Layla, protect her."

Buddy let out an exasperated huff.

"What?" said Tom. "I'm not paying you enough all of a sudden?"

"Not everything is about money."

"If you're worried about dying in some faraway land hunting a dangerous creature, then you're in the wrong line of work."

"I'm not concerned about myself. My life ended a long time ago, you know that. But you gave it back to me. So let me return the favour and save yours."

"You've saved me plenty of times."

"I've saved you every time. Not that I'm keeping tabs. Now, keep behind me."

Buddy stalked forward, raising the bullpup rifle. Tom had no choice but to follow. He sure as shit wasn't going to go off by himself, regardless of how much he rated his ability against miscellaneous monsters.

He hasn't saved me every time, he sulked.

"Help!" shouted someone from among some tents. "Oh my God, what is that thing?"

That's a pretty good indicator of the yeti's presence.

Buddy turned to head in that direction. Tom tapped his shoulder, shook his head when Buddy looked back.

"Layla's tent is over there," he said. He knew this because he'd gotten Buddy to follow her and find out. Not that he'd ever had any intention of heading there in the middle of the night, uninvited. But these were extenuating circumstances, surely.

Buddy jabbed an angry finger in the opposite direction. "Yeti first—it can't kill her if *we* kill *it*."

No, but I want to be seen saving her, thought Tom.

Buddy must have read his mind, as he rolled his eyes. "Meanwhile, while you're pissing around, people you don't happen to want to fuck are being killed by a monster."

"You've grown a conscience all of a sudden?" asked Tom. "A moment ago you wanted to hide in the tent."

"Hide you, who I'm paid to protect, in a tent. But if we're out here anyway, may as well shoot the monster before it does too much harm, eh?"

A terrible tearing sound broke a momentary silence, followed by a gross gulping noise like a dog lapping up water.

"I think it's a bit late for that," said Tom.

"The yeti's busy eating. We can get the drop on it," said Buddy, jabbing forward with two fingers, a military signal from his past life.

"Alright, you go left and I go right."

"How about I go front and you try not to get yourself fucking killed."

"Sounds like a plan."

***

They stalked forward through the tents. People were running everywhere, the beams of their flashlights blinding Tom every time they passed, jumping out of their skins, thinking he or Buddy were the yeti. They invariably would run on, whimpering in fear, not knowing where to go. The terrified mountaineers seemed to take no comfort at all that there were two armed men heading towards that which they feared.

I suppose they think we're just going to get ourselves killed.

The lights started to turn off, the screaming and shouting dying down as people realised there was nowhere to run, only hide. They crawled up where they could, hoping the yeti found someone else, satiated its hunger on them instead.

That's assuming there is a limit to its appetite. It might go on killing until no one is left. Or perhaps when it has got revenge on me for its ruined face, then it will go?

Tom shook his head in the darkness.

There's no way it remembers me after all these years, I'm being stupid. But then again, why has it come this far down the mountain?

The answer to that was obvious. Strewn all over the rocky ground were bodies and parts of bodies ripped to pieces, blood splashed against the plastic tents, shining black in the pale moonlight. From up ahead, around the far side of the large dining tent, came the sound of bones being broken, accompanied by guttural grunts. Tom started to shake. He was reliving a familiar memory in real time, approaching the scene of his father's death. It was everything he could do to put one foot after the other. The rifle in his hand felt like dead weight, a curse that was going to get him killed.

Buddy had his own rifle tucked in tight against his shoulder, barrel pointing where he looked. He stalked forward with careful, quiet steps like a predator in long grass, trying to get the drop on his prey. Tom was being pulled along in his wake as if by a rope tied around their waist.

He's going to drag me to my death like those two Sherpas that fell down the ice rift up on the mountain.

He wanted to say something, to tell Buddy to stop, turn around, but it was too late. If he spoke now the yeti would be alerted to their presence. The dining tent they approached would prove no barrier—it would charge through it, killing hands raised, murder in its eyes. Seconds later, Tom would be nothing more than a hunk of dead meat.

Then I really will be just like my father.

Buddy took a final glance back at his employer. Tom knew he could not see his fear—they were both nothing but black silhouettes against the tent's side—but there was no denying the stench of terror which filled the air.

A sniffing sound—it was the yeti sampling that scent. Buddy's head snapped around. There was no question now of going back. Tom tensed, gripped his rifle tight.

With a bellowed war cry, Buddy jumped around the corner and fired.

19

Bang, bang, bang, bang, bang.

The noise boxed Tom around the ears so hard he was almost too shocked to follow Buddy around the corner. He forced his arms and legs into action, working the bolt of the .303 fluidly and raising it to his shoulder as he took a few unconscious steps forward. The muzzle flashes of Buddy's austeyr lit up the night like a strobe light as he fired on fully automatic. In those isolated frames of illumination, Tom saw the demon from his nightmare staring back at him with one baleful eye, one half of its face a ruined crater.

Tom felt a strong hand squeeze his heart and a spear of cold iron get shoved up his butt as fear nearly overwhelmed him. The yeti stood on a pile of dismembered corpses barely recognisable as human. Its fur was completely drenched in gore, stained red and dripping. Bullets cut up the snow around its hairy feet in a flurry of white. Buddy corrected his fire, the shots stitching upwards in slow motion. Tom also took aim, ready to make the kill shot.

Right in the other half of your face, you evil fucker, he thought, tensing his finger on the trigger as he zeroed in on the remaining eye. It glistened with life in a flashing flare of light. Then there was a split second of darkness before the next shot of Buddy's rifle. When it came, lighting up the scene again, the yeti was gone.

"What the actual…" said Tom, lowering his weapon. A cold shiver passed over him as if he had witnessed something supernatural.

Buddy, more pragmatic, darted forward, panning his rifle left and right. Seeing nothing, he activated a flashlight attached to his chest. "Come and get me, you lumbering oaf. You think I haven't killed fuckers bigger than you before?"

"Careful," said Tom, gathering himself. "It's dangerous."

"No fucking shit." Buddy kicked a human torso, its legs, arms, and head missing, the ribcage cracked open. It tumbled down the scree of snow, spilling blood and organs as it went.

"Where's it gone?" said Tom.

Buddy lifted a hand. "Shh!"

They waited, the time ticking past one heavy, thudding heartbeat at a time. A scream cut the silence on the far side of the camp. Buddy took off after it. Tom had no choice but to rush after him, nearly going head over heels into the snow, slipping on the gore-drenched ground and only regaining his balance with some undignified wind-milling of his arms. Cursing roundly, he trotted on, scanning between the tents, ready for anything, fully expecting the monster to try to flank them.

Don't forget it's come for me, he thought, breathing hard now from the running and the fear.

A silhouette darted at him from the side, cutting between him and Buddy. Tom raised his rifle to blow the thing's head off, only pulling back at the last second. The shape shone a torch in his eyes, dazzling him, but not before he caught a glimpse of a face.

"Layla?" he asked, lifting a hand to shield his sight. She swung the torch away, shining it all directions, turning on the spot over and over. Her eyes were wide with terror.

"That… that *thing* killed my whole team," she managed to say around panicked, sucking breaths.

"It's the yeti."

She looked at him like he was mad.

Or perhaps she fears she's gone mad, thought Tom.

She shook her head, not wanting to believe him, but he nodded, slowly and evenly, and she eventually started to nod along with him.

"I saw it," she admitted. "It's a monster."

"It's an animal like any other." He hefted his rifle. "It can be killed." He felt braver for having to provide comfort for her. But then he noticed he had lost track of Buddy and he doubled over with a pang of terror like a punch to the stomach.

"Are you alright?" asked Layla.

"Ah, yeah," he said, scrambling to recover his dignity. "Just that curry from earlier."

Wrong answer, idiot, he thought, smiling sheepishly and wishing he could crawl into a hole and die.

"Sir," shouted Buddy, jogging up to the two of them.

A wave of relief washed over Tom. It was visible on Layla's face too, who seemed to take great comfort from Buddy's calm military bearing.

“I see he doesn’t just serve the drinks,” said Layla, indicating Buddy’s assault rifle.

“He’s my hunting partner, too,” said Tom.

Buddy jerked a thumb over his shoulder. “I think you should come take a look at this.”

“You’ve got the trace?”

“You could say that.” Buddy turned and stalked off, head swivelling left and right, rifle held ready. Tom followed after him.

“Wait a minute,” said Layla. “Don’t leave me here.”

“Then come with us,” said Tom.

She crossed her arms as if she was going to argue. Tom shrugged. He hefted his rifle and went after Buddy. He reached a tent where Buddy had turned. There he couldn’t help but glance back at her, knowing he was nothing but a dark shadow to her now and she couldn’t see that his nonchalance was an act. Torch clenched in her fist, she straightened her arms by her sides, trotting on the spot like she needed to pee. With a last twist of her head left and right, searching for any alternative and finding none, she gave the snow a petulant kick and hurried after them.

Tom smiled and darted forward, knowing she would follow.

***

The yeti wasn’t hard to track. Buddy led them first to a tent which had been ripped open, its plastic fabric shredded like the wrapping of a kid’s present on Christmas morning. The sleeping occupants had only held the yeti's attention for a few moments—their guts gored out but not chewed up—before it had discarded them like unwanted toys.

"It took the head of that one," said Tom, pointing at one of the corpses.

"A snack to munch on," said Buddy.

Layla projectile vomited all over the decapitated body.

"That curry not agreeing with you either," said Tom, now enjoying her discomfort, able to push his own fear aside in his desire to seem nonplussed by all this.

Just another day in the office for a cryptid collector, he thought. *Bet you feel stupid for not believing me now, eh?*

He chuckled at this.

"You think this is fucking funny?" she said, wiping the puke from her lips. Tom grimaced. She wasn't exactly looking as lovely in this moment as she had before.

"There's a certain dark humour to this line of work," he said in his defence.

"You're both fucking psychos if this is your line of work," she said, her face drained of all colour.

"That's not even the best bit," said Buddy without irony. "Come look at this."

"Oh, joy."

Buddy crunched through the snow, angling the flashlight attached to his chest downwards and indicating the huge footprints with the barrel of his rifle.

"Look at the size of those," said Layla, jaw hanging. "Have you ever seen anything like that?"

"Yes," said Tom.

"Right, I forgot you're old friends with this thing."

"More like old adversaries."

"It's a long term relationship is all I'm saying."

"If so it ends here."

"No, it ends *here*," said Buddy, standing on a lip of icy rock. Tom and Layla struggled up to join him, slushy snow mixed with blood cascading over the rocks, making them slippery. Discarded human bones snapped beneath their boots.

"What the hell am I looking at?" said Layla as she and Tom stood beside Buddy. The butler was grim-faced as he shone his torch down into the wide abyss which opened up before them.

"It's a big yeti hole," said Tom.

Buddy and Layla played their lights about, their beams intersecting and diverging as they traced the dimensions of the hole, scanned down its rock walls, slick with translucent ice which caught the light, sparkling like diamonds.

"We're not going down there, are we?" asked Layla.

"We're not that mad," said Tom.

Layla slumped in relief as Buddy started laughing, the sound echoing down the hole, bouncing back at them like the yeti was hiding down there, mocking them.

As indeed it probably is, thought Tom.

"We need special equipment to go down there," he said. "We'll wait until dawn, take stock of the situation, and then we'll head on in."

"So you are mad," said Layla.

"We're not mad enough to rush in at night. But madness is relative."

Buddy was cackling like a lunatic now, gripping his sides.

"I can see that," said Layla, brows furrowed in genuine concern.

20

First light did not unveil a pleasant scene. Flattened tents dotted the landscape in colourful patches. Snow was all around—a product of the avalanche the yeti had called down in the night and which came right up to the camp. Dead bodies and bits of bodies were to be found everywhere, their discovery often serendipitous like Easter eggs hidden around a garden—a head jammed under a rock, a leg hanging from an antenna, a hand that seemed to have crawled of its own volition into an overturned pot and now resembled a hermit crab.

"You should eat something," Tom said to Layla as they sat perched on a boulder. He wasn't hungry himself but felt he should at least try to take care of her.

"So I can just throw it up again?" she snapped. She had bags under her eyes, her face sagging under the strain of the horror they had witnessed, the evidence of which was still all around them.

"At least have some coffee, ma'am," said Buddy, back playing the part of a proper butler once more, though his rifle was slung across his back, ready for him to switch back to attack dog in an instant. He held the steaming mug out to Layla. She took it, cradled it in her hands for warmth, but didn't drink.

"Thank you," said Tom, taking his own mug. He could at least down some coffee, his addiction to caffeine overcoming even the horror gnawing at his guts.

Still, it's nothing new, is it? If I didn't want to see stuff like this I should never have returned for the yeti. I knew what it is capable of.

He looked around at the other survivors of the night's carnage. The mountaineers stumbled around like zombies amidst the devastation, some seeking out the scattered remains of their friends and companions for identification or burial, others packing up their gear, getting ready to leave, the mountain and its ascent forgotten.

I put all these people in danger by coming back here.

"You can't blame yourself, sir," said Buddy, reading his master's mind. Tom looked up at him hopefully, his eyes shining with fresh tears.

"I can blame him," Layla cut in.

Buddy scowled, shook his head. "It's a wild beast. It does what it wants, attacks indiscriminately."

"Like you two. Just carving a path of destruction across the world, eh?"

"We're here to kill it, to make sure it can't do this again." Buddy indicated a row of dead bodies that had been lined up in the centre of the camp, tarps placed over them.

"You're here for your macabre museum of freak genetics bullshit."

Tom found himself nodding along with this.

"Someone's got to do it," he said absently, staring forward.

"No one has to do this," said Layla. "You could leave the yeti alone and it would leave you alone. But no, you've got to poke the bear, don't you?"

She jabbed him with her finger. "Poke, poke, poke. And when the beast turns at bay, kills your father, kills *near everyone in this whole camp of innocent fucking people*, you just go, oh, whoops, how did that happen? What a mystery—like it has nothing to do with you."

"It knows we're hunting it," Tom conceded.

"Yes, didn't you get that from your own fucked up story about going after it with your father? It knows you're after it, and *in self-defence* it strikes back, luring you on into a trap. That thing is not only dangerous, it's intelligent, and that makes it doubly dangerous."

"She's right, sir," said Buddy. "I inspected that hole we found. It's probably a natural cavern. It must have been covered when we arrived. The yeti brought the avalanche down not to bury us in snow, but to reveal that entrance to its lair."

"Why?" asked Tom.

"To strike at us, give us a prod to stir us up, get us mad so we do something rash and stupid. I think it's trying to lure us into that cave."

"It would fit with its M.O., the way it turned the tables on my father and I."

"So what's the plan?"

"We're going in after it anyway."

Layla let out a snort of disgust. "You're going to get me killed."

"You don't have to come."

"Yes I do." She seemed disappointed in herself, as if destiny had dealt her a bad hand but she had no choice but to play it. "Because I'm a journalist and this is the story of a lifetime."

"It might be the end of your lifetime if you come." He put a protective arm around her shoulders. She shrugged it off.

"I'd never forgive myself if I didn't take this chance. This could be my big break."

"There's very little fame to be had in cryptids, believe me."

"Shut up. You talk about your legacy. Well, this is my chance to secure my own."

She stood up, gave herself a shake as if sloughing off the trauma of the previous night. "Maybe I will have some breakfast, Buddy. I'll need my strength."

21

Tom was packing up gear, getting ready for their descent into the cave, when a fresh group arrived in the camp. Leading them was a stocky man, with deeply lined leathery skin. He marched straight up to Tom and extended a hand, his face creasing around a wide smile.

"Master Tom, good to see you again," said Tenzing.

Tom laughed with happiness, the Sherpa's smile infectious. He slapped his palm into Tenzing's and shook his hand heartily. "It's great to see you, old friend."

"I see you've not aged a day. Your face is as boyish as ever."

"Me? You look exactly the same."

And indeed it seemed as if Tenzing had been kept on ice for the two decades since he had last seen him.

"Time marches for us all, death waiting at its end," said Tenzing.

Tom indicated the camp, still in disarray, burial parties carrying bodies. "Tell me about it."

"What happened here?" Tenzing looked around as if noticing the scene for the first time. He pursed his lips together in a hard, thin line, his nostrils flaring. "I smell yeti."

"Yes, the yeti. I know I gave you a call about a climb a few weeks ago, though it went to voicemail.

Things have changed since then, but I still need your help."

"I am sorry for the delay. I got your message only two days ago. I was busy on another mountain guiding a team of Germans."

"That's okay. You're here now, and just in time."

"You want to begin your ascent today?"

"Descent."

Tenzing frowned.

Tom laughed. "Here, I'll show you."

***

Tenzing and Tom joined Buddy, who was staring at the hole as if willing it to give up its secrets.

"Tenzing, this is Buddy. Buddy, Tenzing," said Tom.

Tenzing extended a hand and they shook firmly.

"I've heard a lot about you," said Buddy with a thin-lipped smile which did not reach his eyes.

"I cannot say the same, I am afraid," said Tenzing, his voice flat and matter-of-fact.

The smile on Buddy's face turned into a toothy grimace as the two men continued to shake hands, their grip getting tighter each moment, their eyes locked. Tenzing's face was that of the rocky mountain, cold and silent.

Tom shifted awkwardly—it was like watching a pit bull and a rottweiler square off.

"So what do you make of this?" he asked Tenzing, jerking his head at the hole.

Tenzing broke Buddy's grip, knelt down to inspect the opening in the earth. Buddy shot Tom a look.

Be angry if you like, Buddy, thought Tom. *But I need all the expert help I can get on this one. Your pride will have to take the hit.*

"Pretty standard yeti cave," said Tenzing after a while, running his finger along the icy rim of the hole. "Though I didn't know they dug them this far down the mountain."

"Yeti cave?" asked Tom.

"Yes, most of them are on the Tibetan side of the range. The monks use the abandoned ones for meditation retreats."

"You never mentioned anything like that the last time we met."

"I told your father. He did not believe me. And I didn't get the feeling you were all that interested in the yeti. How things change." He shook his head, as if saddened by Tom's choices.

Yet he's still back here to help me, thought Tom.

"I was more concerned with staying alive," he said.

"Ah," said Tenzing, standing, "then it was lucky you had me to carry you back down the mountain."

"You didn't carry me. I remember doing some hobbling of my own."

"I lowered you on the ropes, dragged you along on a tarp." Tenzing picked up a small rock, threw it down the hole like a coin down a wishing well. "Though you did give me a big tip at the end."

Ah, so that's why he's back, thought Tom.

"But I did not do it for money," said Tenzing. "I did it because that expedition had seen enough death." He swept his arm around as if to indicate the whole camp. "Has this expedition not seen enough death already?"

"We're determined to go," said Buddy, his jaw set.

"Is this so?" Tenzing asked Tom directly.

Buddy bristled. Tom nodded.

"I will not ask my men to come," said Tenzing. "I am still haunted by the loss of my team that day on the mountain, though over two decades have passed. But I will go with you, if only to help you confront that which so obviously tortures you, Master Tom."

"Thanks, Tenzing."

Tenzing smacked his lips as if he had just taken a refreshing drink. "Of course, the tip will be truly generous, and I will finally retire, spend my days enjoying my grandchildren."

"You can name your price."

"Tsk, tsk, such things are not polite." He winked. "But I shall take what you think is fair."

"Buddy here will make the arrangements."

"And I will ready my climbing gear. The ice walls of this hole are steep. We'll have to employ a lot of the same technique as we would when descending the mountain." He stretched his back, limbering up. "I am getting old, regardless of what you say. I had thought this would be my last journey up the mountain, but down into it will be a nice change. It will test my courage and afterwards I can rest easy, knowing I have lived my life to the full."

"You said this has been dug out?" asked Buddy, his professional bearing returned, the military man getting his intel in line before an assault.

Tenzing smiled at him like he knew and understood such men, that he was one himself, rugged and practical. "It is not natural. The yeti carves them out of the earth to move undetected. How do you think they have avoided mankind so successfully for so long?"

"It used this one to get close to the camp," said Buddy. "It got the jump on us."

"Tom knows how cunning they can be."

"Don't remind me," said Tom.

"Best you remember, or this hole will be our grave."

"It was the same yeti which killed my father."

Tenzing raised his eyebrows, impressed. "You saw it?"

"It had half its face blown off."

"Then it wants you dead." Tenzing jabbed a finger into the hole. "And it is willing to go to great lengths to make that happen."

"As are we," said Buddy.

22

Tenzing laid his climbing equipment out near the edge of the hole. There were great lengths of rope, carabiners, ice picks, crampons, and more.

"We've got plenty of this stuff ourselves," said Buddy.

Tenzing kept working without looking up. "I trust my gear. I don't know your gear."

"Ours is the best money can buy."

"This gear has saved my life countless times. It has proven its worth, more than money."

"Money buys quality."

"Money buys illusions of quality. Money buys a brand name."

"Those companies have a pedigree. You're just being obtuse."

Tenzing slapped a coiled rope emphatically. "I trust my gear."

"Let him use his gear, Buddy," said Tom. "Not everything is a pissing contest."

"Yes, *sir*," said Buddy, and went to go over the weapons, rations, and other gear, something that made him feel useful and comfortable. He was soon humming happily to himself.

"That is an odd man," Tenzing said to Tom.

"He is, but very experienced. He's saved my life plenty of times."

"He's a military man?"

"Ex-French foreign legion."

"I don't know much about it."

"They're tough."

Tenzing nodded once. "So are the Sherpa people."

"I need you two to work together."

"I am a professional."

"We all are."

Tenzing laughed. "Professional yeti hunter. Your father just did it as a hobby."

"No one's paying me to do this, so I suppose it's a hobby for me, too."

"A deadly serious one."

"No more than climbing the mountain, or jumping down an ice hole, for that matter. We're abseiling down I assume."

"Yes."

"You've only got three harnesses."

"Only three people."

"There's a fourth. A woman. Her name is Layla."

"Oh? Another professional?" Tenzing teased.

"A journalist."

"Ah, I see. Tom the *famous* yeti hunter. Your father was also a glory hog. Look where that got him."

"Life's too short not to face your fears."

"I agree. I do not like confined spaces."

"You're claustrophobic?"

"I have lived my whole life out on the mountains, under the open sky."

"You did well when we were buried in that hole after the avalanche, all those years ago."

"Where do you think I developed my fear?"

"And you think you'll banish the past by going down that hole?"

Tenzing fixed him a serious look. "Don't you?"

***

"You're surprisingly good at this," Tom said to Layla as they abseiled down the icy walls of the hole side by side. The opening was big enough for a yeti—it easily fit two people.

"That's very condescending," she said, making another smooth, gliding jump, digging her crampons in as she landed. He did the same.

"It was a compliment."

"You expected me to be hopeless? I'm part of a team that's climbing Mount Everest."

"*Was* climbing Everest," he corrected, instantly regretting it as she turned the headlamp of her torch on him, the light like a single, burning eye.

He squinted. "Sorry."

"You should be, you insensitive idiot. Seems like your party is the only one where the yeti *didn't* kill anyone."

"Because we had the sense to bring guns."

"Everyone else was on a peaceful expedition. They didn't know they *needed* guns. And did you warn them of the danger?"

"I honestly thought the camp was safe, that we'd find the yeti up the mountain, if at all."

She pushed off again, the rope whining through her metal alloy descender. Once again he followed. Above, the entrance to the hole looked like a shining coin held at arm's length. Below was a fathomless abyss.

I hope Tenzing measured the depth right. I'd hate to run out of rope.

"And then what happens?" asked Layla.

"Then what happens when?"

"In your hypothetical ideal scenario where you're up the mountain, shooting at the damned thing, causing avalanches and other havoc, getting innocent people killed."

I've already done that, thought Tom sourly, visions of the camp coming back to haunt him.

"Ah," he said, knowing he had no defence.

"Exactly, you're a selfish, egotistical maniac."

"Sounds like standard rich guy stuff."

She laughed with a wild abandon as she made another leap into the darkness. "But at least you're not boring."

***

They touched down on rocky ground, slick with ice.

"Well, that's a relief," said Tom.

"What?" asked Layla. She shone her headlamp around the small cavern.

"I thought the yeti would be here waiting to jump out and butcher us the second we got to the bottom."

"Oh, great. Why didn't you let Buddy go first with his assault rifle if you thought that was the case?"

Tom jabbed a thumb into his chest. “Hey, I’m the one leading here.”

“Off you go then, fearless leader. I’ll wait for the others.” She jutted her chin at an opening in the wall. It wasn’t large. They’d have to stoop to enter it.

“You want me to go in there?” he asked.

“It’s the only other way out, the only way forward.”

“I’ll wait for Buddy. I need backup.”

“Exactly, why take the risk when you can send an employee in?”

“Buddy loves the danger. This stuff is fun for him.”

“And you?”

He shrugged. “It gets the heart going.”

“You’re both fucked up in the head. Your day job must be boring.”

“I own mines.”

“This is right up your alley then,” she said, kicking some rocks. “I thought your father had factories? That’s what you said in your story.”

“I tried to make it work, even got my degree in chemistry.”

“Not in business?”

“They were chemical factories. I wanted to understand the environmental impact our company had.”

“So you got out of that and into mining? Far out, that must have taken some mental gymnastics.”

“After university I travelled a lot. I was backpacking through Australia—that’s where I met

Buddy—and I saw there was a lot of money to be made there in mining."

"The money wins out in the end, right?"

"I had a lot to prove, taking over my dad's wealth at such a young age. So I took a huge gamble, sold my stake in the factories, bought into mines. I turned my father's fortune of a hundred million pounds into a billion dollars in twenty years."

"So you're a true to life billionaire then?"

"Australian dollars, but yes."

"But not in the States?"

"No, there I'm just considered exceedingly wealthy."

"What do you two think you're doing?" hissed Buddy as he landed beside them. He unclipped from the rope and raised his rifle in a single fluid motion. "Having a good old chat?"

"No sir or ma'am this time?" sneered Layla.

"Do I have to remind you there's a damned yeti down here?"

"It's not here, Buddy," said Tom. "You can calm down."

"I can calm down when I'm dead, which is exactly what we'll all be if you two don't take this more seriously. You can flirt when this is over."

"We're not flirting," Tom and Layla said at the same time.

Tenzing landed with a thud, tumbled over ungracefully. "I'm better at going up," he said as Tom helped him to his feet.

"Let's move out. I'm on point," said Buddy, crouching down to enter the tunnel leading out of the cavern.

Tom looked at Laya, who raised her eyebrows at him. "No," he said. "This is my hunt. I'll go first."

He unslung the Lee-Enfield off his back and stalked forward.

23

The tunnel was a dismal place, cold, wet, slippery, and dark. Tom didn't like to use his headlamp—knowing it warned the yeti they were coming—but he had no choice. Every now and then the tunnel branched off, and that included big holes in the ground which could swallow a man without warning.

At each of these intersections, they paused, huddled in a group, ears straining for any sound made by the yeti. Invariably Tenzing would eventually indicate one or another of the offshoots.

"That way," he'd say with certainty, though Tom didn't know how he knew, though he suspected.

Smells like yeti. That is what he'd said on the surface.

Once more he was in awe of the superhuman abilities of the Sherpa.

There was another thing which guided them on. Every now and then, they heard a distant, muffled yodelling which made the walls vibrate, shaking flakes of ice loose from the ceiling.

"What do you think that means?" asked Tom.

"A warning?" suggested Layla.

"A threat," said Buddy with grim certainty.

Tenzing shook his head. "They're talking. They know we are here."

"They?"

"Yes," said Tenzing, sniffing loudly like a hound. "There are two of them."

***

"I see something up ahead," whispered Buddy, who had naturally filtered to the front of the group with Tenzing. Tom hung at the back with Layla, pretending he was protecting her, or perhaps watching their vulnerable rear.

As long as she doesn't think I'm a coward, he thought. He needn't have worried—Layla looked scared enough for the two of them. She was also distracted by something on the ground. She nudged him without looking up, her headlamp trained on an object which caught the light with the flashing sheen of a turning blade.

It was a bone.

"Human?" he asked. The yellowed femur clinked on the ice as he gave it a kick.

"Looks too big for human," she said.

"It's a yeti bone," said Tenzing, who had doubled back. He picked it up and inspected it. The thing was stout like a baseball bat, thick at both ends, one forking into two nubs, the other a knobbly sphere of bone. Tenzing slapped the ball joint of the thing into his palm with a whack. "This would make a good club."

"The yeti isn't a caveman. It's a monster," said Tom.

"I never said otherwise. It's not a tool. At least, we've not seen the yeti use it as such."

"So what's it doing here?"

"Turn your bloody lights off!" hissed Buddy. He said it with such insistence they instantly complied, the dread gloom closing in on them. But while the darkness was oppressive and ominous, it wasn't total. There was a faint blue-white glow up ahead at the end of the tunnel, with Buddy silhouetted against it as he shuffled forward.

"Do we follow?" asked Layla.

"Let him do his job," said Tom.

"What if he needs help?"

"Tenzing, go with him, see what's down there."

"I thought you were leading?" goaded Layla.

"I am. I'm delegating."

She snorted in derision.

"If you're so keen, ladies first," said Tom.

He heard Layla shifting around in the darkness, as if deciding which was more important, her pride or self-preservation. She surprised Tom by shoving him to the side, Tenzing as well, and heading down the tunnel, her hunching form blocking the source of light.

"We may as well go too," said Tom, suddenly feeling isolated and alone, despite the sound of Tenzing's calm breathing beside him.

"Ladies first," teased Tenzing.

***

Layla and Buddy were blocking the end of the tunnel, so it wasn't immediately apparent what they were looking at or why they had stopped.

"What is—" began Tom, but Tenzing's hand clamped over his mouth to silence him.

"You cannot smell *that*?" asked the Sherpa in a barely audible whisper directly into his ear. He released his hand. Tom took a deep breath, smelt the carnal stink of decay and old rot. Buddy looked back at him, nodding in agreement with the look of dawning horror on Tom's face.

I still don't know what it is, though, thought Tom, crawling forward, careful where he placed his hands and knees. A pale blue light filtered around Layla and Buddy, brighter now, yet somehow more diffused, like the light in a glass house, soft and mellow, at odds with the tang of death which stabbed up Tom's nostrils and caught in the back of his throat. Layla leant back to make way for him to look, though she didn't take her eyes off whatever lay beyond, as if she were committing it to memory for later description in her article.

I bet she's pissed off I wouldn't let her bring a camera, he thought as he peered over her shoulder. But such petty concerns vanished as he caught sight of what she saw, his mind reeling. Before him was a scene of great beauty juxtaposed with terrible horror. Tom's eyeballs shuddered in their sockets—he had to rub them to make them focus again.

The cavern stretching out before them was large, far larger than any they had yet come across—so large it would have been impossible for the yeti to excavate and must have been formed long ago by natural forces. It had two distinct and awe-inspiring features beyond its great size.

The first was the ceiling. It was like that of a massive cathedral, vaulted and beautiful in ornamentation and design. But where a cathedral's ceiling would be handcrafted by talented artisans, the cave's was formed by time and ice. Stalactites hung in vast abundance, intricately arrayed as if arranged by the hand of God for maximum beauty. They were like spears delicately suspended in the air as if by magic, their points sharp and threatening. The whole looming mass of them looked as deadly as they did stunning.

Adding to the visual spectacle was the diffused light shining through from beyond this frozen barrier, which made the icy stalactites glow the faint blue he had seen before. Tom could only assume the light was that of the sun, filtering down through a thick layer of ice, its illumination diffusing throughout the cavern, providing etheric blue light by which to see the cave's other defining feature.

Tom's eyes dropped to it, his vision tunnelling in terror as he tried to take it in, the scope of it as dreadful as the content. The floor of the cavern was a field of bones. The sight of them made Tom's heart thump in terror, the blue glow making them seem eerie, like the skeletons of ghosts. Stalagmites, smaller than their cousins on the ceiling, yet no less sharp and ominous, stabbed up around and through the bones, as if whatever creatures the skeletons had belonged to had been impaled on their grievous spikes. It took Tom a long while to conceive of the scale of what he was looking at. The bones were so thickly laid he could not see the ground beneath. What's more, the bones were *big*—not human at all.

"Yeti bones," said Tenzing, his words sounding like an evil invocation of a voodoo sorcerer.

Layla let out a high-pitched squeak, as if she wanted to scream but her throat was too tightly pinched in terror to do so.

"What is this, a yeti graveyard?" asked Buddy.

Tenzing grunted, not in assent but annoyance, as if this was stating the obvious.

"That's a lot of dead yetis," said Tom with a heavy gulp.

"And one living one!" said Buddy, rising from a crouch, swinging his assault rifle up. He darted forward, crunching the ancient bones to dust beneath his boots.

"No, stop," said Tenzing, jumping forward, trying to catch the man, his gloved hand finding nothing but air.

Buddy fired as he ran, his rifle spitting fiery spears of light which traced across the cavern, pointing out his target. On the far side of the cavern was another opening, much like that of the tunnel in which Tom crouched, though bigger. Framed in this circular aperture was a now familiar, yet horrifying sight.

The yeti stood with arms spread like a warrior inviting the challenge of a rival. Bullets ricocheted off the rock around it, but it did not flinch. Instead, it beat its chest with meaty thumps like an ominous drum.

Tom got up with a start, knowing something was wrong, however. He switched on his headlamp, trained it on the beast. It squinted, more phased by this than Buddy's rifle fire.

"It's not the yeti," said Tom.

"Sure looks like one," said Layla. She was pressed flat against the wall of the tunnel, trying to keep out of sight.

"No, I mean it's not *the* yeti. This one has its face intact. It's not the one which attacked the camp, the one which killed my father."

Buddy kept charging, correcting his fire, this time slicing a shot through the yeti's elbow. It howled in pain, the sound so loud and monstrous it made the stalactites overhead rock back and forth like chandeliers during an earthquake.

"Get back, you fool," said Tenzing, running after Buddy.

Tom raised his own rifle, working the bolt in a familiar ritual which steadied his nerves. He lined the yeti up in the iron sights, snapped off a shot. It punched through the beast's thigh.

"Damn it, that should have been an easy shot," he said, chiding himself. He worked the bolt, watching Buddy get in close while he did so, firing from the hip on semi-automatic.

Tenzing was still chasing after him. The Sherpa watched the ceiling as he ran, not the ground, and he tripped on a stalagmite, tumbling forward into the bones, which crumbled under his weight, thrown up into the air like dust.

Buddy's fire cut up the wall around the yeti, scoring another glancing shot across its shoulder and peppering it with shattered rock fragments.

Why isn't it running away? Tom asked himself. *And if not that, why not charge Buddy, close the gap between them and attempt to rip the man apart?*

He got his answer right away. The yeti gave its chest one final pound with its gargantuan fist and sucked in a breath. Opening its mouth wide, it gave vent to a warbling note of terrific volume and intensity. The air vibrated. The bones on the floor rattled as if they were alive, adding their collective voice to the cacophony. Above, the stalactites shook like the spears of a massed warrior host.

Tenzing rolled over in the trembling field of bones just in time to see one of the stalactites shake loose, fall directly at him. It stabbed him right through the face with a sickening slice. Another impaled his body, flesh parting as if to a steel blade. More followed, but the Sherpa was already dead. The heavy stalactites shattered like struck ice sculptures as they pinned his corpse down into the pulverised bones, burying him beneath their weight so he disappeared from sight.

The last Tom saw of Buddy he was still charging forward through the deluge of falling stalactites, firing from the hip, a bellowed war cry on his lips to match the yodelling shout of the yeti. The monster stood defiant before him, taking further fire from Buddy as he closed the last few metres. Then, he too, disappeared behind a final thick curtain of stalactites shaken loose from the ceiling. They shattered all across the cavern like a ceiling of glass brought down in a horrifying rain of broken glass shards.

Tom let his rifle hang on its sling. With one arm he shielded his face, with the other he put an arm out to pull Layla away from the tunnel mouth. She fell into his arms and he held her tight. She screamed, but the sound of it was lost in the deafening noise of the cavern's ceiling coming down. Even the yeti's yodelling could no longer be heard. Nor could Tom hear Buddy's firing.

They're dead, then, he thought, but felt no triumph at the death of the yeti and no sadness at the loss of Buddy or Tenzing. His own life hung in the balance. Adrenaline pumped through his body as flying shards of ice as big as a butcher's cleaver careened past his head, exploding upon impact with the walls and filling the tunnel with deadly, frozen shrapnel. He hardly felt the pain as they cut up his skin, trying to wrap Layla up protectively in his arms. All they could do was shut their eyes and run as one, slipping and skidding on the icy rocks beneath their feet, but kept upright by sheer will and the desire to live. They couldn't hear their own screaming over the whoosh of air and sound of exploding ice.

Only when the roar died down did Tom realise they'd stopped running, clear of the frozen debris which had chased them down the tunnel. For a second all was darkness—his eyes still squeezed shut. As he opened them he expected to find some meagre comfort in the light of his headlamp and with it the sight of Layla, clutched in his arms.

Instead, he was greeted by a monstrously proportioned face so close to his own he could feel the moist heat of its breath on his skin. Its features were shattered and broken by a grievous wound of twisted flesh, exposing the internal cavities of its skull like an anatomy class cadaver. A single remaining eye stared with burning hatred, wide and bloodshot. In the other socket was nothing but a dark abyss. The tunnel was filled with the carnal stench of dried gore twisted into wet fur, emanating from a hulking body which shuffled its huge feet.

Tom’s mind exploded with terror-inducing recognition. The yeti that killed his father was there in the tunnel with them. And now it was going to kill him too.

24

This time Tom did hear Layla scream, for there was no other noise in the tunnel besides the monster's terrible grunting breaths. Her cry was a piercing shriek of mortal terror, ramming into his eardrum like an iron spike.

The pain of it saved them.

Reflexively Tom pushed Layla away. She stumbled and fell backward into a side tunnel set at a downwards angle from the first, and went tumbling away as if down a children's slide. Her scream became a falling, fading note, punctuated with a thud and silence.

For Tom there was no such easy escape. He only narrowly avoided being squashed into the floor by an overarm strike by the yeti's hammering fist by pressing himself against a wall. This blow was followed a second later by a punch which would have flattened him into the rock if he didn't duck down and dart between the yeti's long legs. He started to run, his headlamp flashing around madly.

What about Layla? She's probably stuck down that tunnel, he thought. *The yeti could—*

He turned to go back, but the yeti was hot on his heels.

Nope, apparently it wants me after all.

His rifle was still slung around his shoulders, dangling around his waist. Taking it in his grip he pulled the trigger of the Lee-Enfield in panic, but didn't even have the barrel pointed back down the tunnel. The shot went off into the ceiling with a loud bang, blasting loose shards of icy rock, coating the yeti. The deafening noise made the beast pause in its tracks, shaking its head. Tom's own ears rung from the concussive blast in the confined space, but he repeated the trick for good measure, further stunning the yeti, giving him enough time to run.

Damn, I should have just shot it in the face.

Further down the tunnel he turned to do this but misjudged the lead he had. The yeti, with its bigger stride, had closed the distance in a few seconds. Now it picked him up like a tidal wave, hurled him forward with terrible force. He tumbled end over end and landed hard, his whole weight going down on the rifle beneath him. It knocked the wind out of him with a wheeze and stars danced before his eyes, but he knew his life was measured in fractions of a second, so he rolled over, swinging the rifle around to aim at the yeti as it bore down on him like an avalanche of crushing whiteness.

The rifle didn't fire when he pulled the trigger. The wooden stock had snapped, the barrel bent out of true. It was useless. He couldn't even swing it as a club, the yeti now too close. Its smashed face came close to his, mouth open wide, its huge, sharp incisors like those of a gorilla, ready to bite down on Tom's head, crush it like a melon.

He closed his eyes and heard a warbling bellow.

That's the last thing I'll ever hear, a damn yeti's cry of feral triumph.

The sound was punctuated by a sharp, tight burst of automatic rifle fire like the sound of tearing cloth. Tom snapped his eyes open. It wasn't the yeti's yodel he'd heard but Buddy's shouted war cry. Bullets stitched up the yeti's chest, horrific wounds opening like blossoming red flowers. The beast roared in agony, its bestial visage mirrored in Buddy's as he roared right back, getting in close and continuing to hose the yeti down.

The beast lifted an arm to strike him, but it lost strength even as it did so. The limb fell limp. Buddy got between Tom and the yeti, shooting the remainder of his clip up at it, ruining what remained of its already shattered face. Then he leapt aside, landing in a commando roll as the yeti tottered, its head a pulped mess.

Tom went wide eyed as he realised the beast was coming down like a tree felled by a logger. He yelped and rolled aside, pressed his prone body against the wall as the yeti landed with a thud, throwing up a spray of gossamer flakes of ice. These danced serenely in the air, sparkling in the light of Tom's headlamp, and came to rest on the back of the dead yeti like a light covering of snow.

"Bloody hell, that was too damned close," said Tom, getting up and dusting himself off. His heart was still pumping wildly, adrenaline coursing painfully around his body, making his skin tingle. Buddy was already on his feet, reloading his rifle and scanning around as if expecting more yetis to jump out of the walls.

Tom looked down at the yeti with regret, not quite believing it was over. "I would have liked to have taken it out myself."

"Maybe some more modern weaponry next time," said Buddy, giving the broken remnants of the Lee-Enfield a kick.

"Hey, that's a family heirloom. Well, it w*as* a family heirloom."

Buddy jutted his chin out at the yeti. "Now just another shattered memory to put behind you."

Tom sighed, feeling no sense of triumph, no release. Absent were these things he anticipated to gain from this exorcism of his nightmares. In their place was only exhaustion. His body shuddered, coming down from the heights of mortal terror. He waved vaguely at the yeti's decapitated corpse as if it were some mess he wanted Buddy to clean up, though there was one final act Tom needed to do for himself.

"Get the vials out, will you? I'll take samples of blood and hair for the collection."

"Yes, sir."

25

The camp had a lot of stone cairns where the mountaineers had buried their dead companions. Tom tried not to count them, knowing their blood was on his hands.

And all so I could add one more number to my collection. What's this mad pursuit going to cost me in the end? Probably more than I can pay.

He gave a generous amount to Tenzing's fellow Sherpas—for the man's family as well as their own trouble.

"It's the least I can do," he said to them as Buddy handed the money over.

Tom shook each of their hands in turn, lost in his own thoughts as he spoke his condolences.

Tenzing saved my life on the mountain, all those years ago, and I threw his away beneath it for nothing. He deserved better.

The Sherpas sang their mourning dirge even as they got to work, lifting the stretcher between them. They carried Layla over the rocky ground towards the waiting helicopter he'd called in on the satellite phone. Her leg was held rigid with a splint, her face pale with pain.

Tom walked alongside, held her hand. "Quite a fall you took down that tunnel," he said.

"It was a pretty crappy date, but I've had worse."

"Maybe we'll go on another when you get better?"

She smiled wanly and closed her eyes, didn't respond. They loaded her into the helicopter. Tom stood back, waving as it took off.

"You didn't want to go with her, sir?" asked Buddy, coming up to stand beside him. Together they watched the helicopter ascend into the clear blue sky.

"No, I don't want to crowd her," said Tom.

"Still think you're in with a shot?"

"I did kill a yeti. If that doesn't impress a girl, I don't know what would."

Buddy cocked an eyebrow at this.

Tom jabbed him in the ribs with an elbow with a laugh. "I couldn't have done it without you, of course."

"Of course, sir."

"That was some trick you pulled, gunning down the first yeti then doubling back around through some side tunnels to flank the second."

"Just basic tactics, sir."

"You were lucky not to be crushed by those stalactites."

"Yes, lucky, sir."

Tom slapped him on the back. "I think you've earned a raise."

Buddy took a slow, deep breath in and out. "It's the least you can do, sir."

Check out other great

Cryptid Novels!

J.H. Moncrieff

RETURN TO DYATLOV PASS

In 1959, nine Russian students set off on a skiing expedition in the Ural Mountains. Their mutilated bodies were discovered weeks later. Their bizarre and unexplained deaths are one of the most enduring true mysteries of our time. Nearly sixty years later, podcast host Nat McPherson ventures into the same mountains with her team, determined to finally solve the mystery of the Dyatlov Pass incident. Her plans are thwarted on the first night, when two trackers from her group are brutally slaughtered. The team's guide, a superstitious man from a neighboring village, blames the killings on yetis, but no one believes him. As members of Nat's team die one by one, she must figure out if there's a murderer in their midst—or something even worse—before history repeats itself and her group becomes another casualty of the infamous Dead Mountain.

Gerry Griffiths

CRYPTID ZOO

As a child, rare and unusual animals, especially cryptid creatures, always fascinated Carter Wilde. Now that he's an eccentric billionaire and runs the largest conglomerate of high-tech companies all over the world, he can finally achieve his wildest dream of building the most incredible theme park ever conceived on the planet... CRYPTID ZOO. Even though there have been apparent problems with the project, Wilde still decides to send some of his marketing employees and their families on a forced vacation to assess the theme park in preparation for Opening Day. Nick Wells and his family are some of those chosen and are about to embark on what will become the most terror-filled weekend of their lives—praying they survive. STEP RIGHT UP AND GET YOUR FREE PASS... TO CRYPTID ZOO

Check out other great

Cryptid Novels!

Hunter Shea

LOCH NESS REVENGE

Deep in the murky waters of Loch Ness, the creature known as Nessie has returned. Twins Natalie and Austin McQueen watched in horror as their parents were devoured by the world's most infamous lake monster. Two decades later, it's their turn to hunt the legend. But what lurks in the Loch is not what they expected. Nessie is devouring everything in and around the Loch, and it's not alone. Hell has come to the Scottish Highlands. In a fierce battle between man and monster, the world may never be the same. Praise for THEY RISE : "Outrageous, balls to the wall...made me yearn for 3D glasses and a tub of popcorn, extra butter!" – The Eyes of Madness "A fast-paced, gore-heavy splatter fest of sharksploitation." The Werd "A rocket paced horror story. I enjoyed the hell out of this book." Shotgun Logic Reviews

C.G. Mosley

BAKER COUNTY BIGFOOT CHRONICLE

Marie Bledsoe only wants her missing brother Kurt back. She'll stop at nothing to make it happen and, with the help of Kurt's friend Tony, along with Sheriff Ray Cochran, Marie embarks on a terrifying journey deep into the belly of the mysterious Walker Laboratory to find him. However, what she and her companions find lurking in the laboratory basement is beyond comprehension. There are cryptids from the forest being held captive there and something...else. Enjoy this suspenseful tale from the mind of C.G. Mosley, author of Wood Ape. Welcome back to Baker County, a place where monsters do lurk in the night!

www.ingramcontent.com/pod-product-compliance
Lightning Source LLC
Chambersburg PA
CBHW061240170626
46809CB00007B/2760

9781923165465